THE
DEMON
KILLER

An enthralling murder mystery with a twist

FRANCES LLOYD

Detective Inspector Jack Dawes Mystery Book 7

JOFFE
BOOKS

Joffe Books, London
www.joffebooks.com

First published in Great Britain in 2021

ISBN: 978-1-78931-736-7

PROLOGUE

Hell is empty and all the devils are here!
William Shakespeare, *The Tempest*

Midnight on a hot, humid Friday in August — the month when this nocturnal demon's attack against man is strongest. He is invoked by necromantic rituals of divination. He knows of past, present and future events, secret things, the liberal black arts, the history of creation and the fall of the angels. As one of the Grand Dukes of Hell, he possesses immense power that must be recognized and feared.

In a secluded clearing in Richington Forest, more than forty acolytes — anonymous in their black hooded robes — had gathered to worship. A circle, burned into the forest floor, marked out the place into which the demon would be summoned. Slowly, the followers, each carrying a black candle, began to shuffle around an ancient chest tomb in the centre of the gathering. The chanting began: '*Ave Satanas* — Hail Satan,' the infernal name invoking the demon to attend the Black Mass. Gradually, the incantation became louder and the circling faster. When the whirling reached fever pitch and the noise rose to a loud crescendo, there was a shout —

'Stop! *In nomine dei nostri Satanas Luciferi Excelsi*. I order you to stop — in the name of our God, Satan, Lucifer of the Most High.'

The throng fell to their knees, as a dark shape emerged from the trees. The goat-headed figure had a man's torso, smooth and muscular, but from the waist down, curly black hair sprouted from the hind legs and cloven hooves of a goat. Between its horns burned a black candle, and as the figure passed around the circle, each worshipper rose up and lit their candle from it.

At the end of this ritual, the goat figure leaped up onto the limestone tomb — the top slab now painted black — and sat, cross-legged. Its eyes glowed like hot coals and green, fetid vapours dribbled from its nostrils. At one end of the slab was a statuette of the devil with an erect phallus, at least thirty centimetres long. At the other end, there stood a human skull, filled with a dark red liquid.

The chant began again: 'Astaroth — Beelzebub — Lucifer — hear us!'

The goat demon stood up, arms outstretched in supplication. Two fingers on each hand pointed up and two pointed down — the devil's horns. 'Within this circle, I call thee. Within this circle, I bind thee. Within this circle, I summon thee. I call thee forth.' Red flames flared upwards from the statuette of Lucifer.

A previously selected member of the congregation — a woman of at least forty, claiming to be a virgin — came forward and slipped off her robe. She was naked underneath, eager for her initiation. The goat figure placed her face down on the tomb and used her bare back as an altar. He recited the sacrament backwards, inverting the crucifix and inviting the celebrants to come forward and drink desecrated wine from the skull. Then, using a blackened turnip slice in place of the host, he put it between the woman's thighs and quickly, in a furtive manner, he dipped it inside her. Rapid copulation followed, lasting only a couple of minutes. Then he raised a black chalice, containing a mixture of semen, vaginal secretions and the woman's urine — an elixir for immortality. The goat blessed the faithful and sprinkled the blasphemous, obscene concoction over the assembly.

This was the signal for the crowd to throw off their robes and gyrate, naked, to hellish music, pulsating from the trees. The dance became a wild orgy, fuelled by alcohol and drugs, until exhausted, they slunk away into the night.

CHAPTER ONE

The convent of St Columbanus stood on a grassy knoll to the south-west of Kings Richington — an affluent, self-satisfied town, nestling beside a quiet stretch of the Thames. The convent had been founded by a group of sisters who came to Kings Richington in the late nineteenth century from a priory in Brussels. The nuns were from the Order of Poor Clares, who aimed to be as self-sufficient as possible. For this reason, the convent was set in thirty acres of parkland, well away from the town, and enclosed by a twelve-foot wall. Within this wall, the nuns lived and died with as little recourse to the outside world as possible. They grew their own food, contrived their own medicines and, when they weren't working or sleeping, devoted their time to prayer.

The convent building, a rambling and rather ugly edifice, was designed over a period of years by a local ecclesiastical architect and was eventually completed in 1875. The many structures on the estate included a lodge, which served as the priest's house, a chapel, several cloister buildings and a quadrangle. At its peak, during the 1940s, the convent was home to more than fifty nuns, but numbers slowly declined over time until it became unsustainable. The convent stood empty for some years and fell into disrepair.

It was finally taken over from the Catholic Church by a New Age movement who called themselves the Foundation of the Free Spirit. In stark contrast to their pious predecessors, the cult believed that individuals and their personal preferences were the primary sources of authority on spiritual matters. This meant the freedom and autonomy to do whatever they pleased — a spirituality without borders or confining dogma. No doubt such permissiveness had the good nuns in the churchyard spinning in their graves.

* * *

Lilith viewed the week's takings with some satisfaction. They were up twenty per cent on the previous week. She ran the financial side of the Foundation while her brother, Solomon, supervised the various activities. The third member of the hierarchy — although the cult professed not to have a central authority — was Urbain. At least, that was the name he called himself, but Lilith had seen papers among his belongings that suggested it was something more mundane, particularly while he had been detained at Her Majesty's pleasure. He claimed it was a name befitting people who were idealistic and intuitive and could inspire others. He could certainly do that. There were many young women living in the Foundation House who were 'inspired' by him on a regular basis. He was, he said, a seeker of spiritual truth and was simply developing his potential. He dismissed any idea that it might be construed as a misuse of power.

The door to the study opened and Solomon strode in. Lilith quickly closed the accounts file on her computer.

'Lilith, I'm worried about that new member — Charlie. He asks too many questions and he's too full of himself — roaring around the grounds on that flashy red motorbike at all hours. What do we know about him?'

Lilith brought up the files containing members' details. 'Not much. You know it's our policy not to enquire too deeply into the affairs of our followers. We promote the

Foundation as "a place to forget your past and start a new life — free from the constraints and anxieties of an oppressive society". Giving them the third degree when they arrive is hardly synonymous with that.' She peered at Charlie's details, which were sparse. 'He said when he applied that his reason for joining the Foundation was for "personal growth". He also made a very vague reference to "learning the powerful sciences", whatever that means. He seems harmless enough and his contributions are regular. That "flashy red motor-bike" is a Harley Davidson and they don't come cheap.'

Solomon frowned. 'Hmm. I still think we should keep an eye on him—' He lowered his voice — 'especially on Friday.'

Lilith waved him away. 'Leave the worrying to me — you just do what you do best.'

* * *

The commune had become established slowly. Members came and went, but there was a core of twelve disciples for whom the New Age way of life was ideal — for a variety of reasons, known only to them. They were an eclectic bunch, many of whom Lilith would not have thought suited to a communal lifestyle but, with a few exceptions, they rubbed along pretty well. Currently, there were over twenty members, which included several recent admissions. Summer, a nervous young woman, was the latest. She claimed to be seventeen but looked much younger. She had arrived at the main gates late at night, begging to be taken in.

'Please, let me in. I don't know where else to go.'

It had been raining quite hard and Lilith had noticed her bedraggled state. She had to have been out in the storm for most of the night and it looked as though she'd had some kind of accident, as there were stains on her jeans that could have been blood.

'Where are your parents?' Lilith had asked her, gently.

'They died when I was young.'

'Don't you have any other relatives who could look after you? This isn't a hotel, it's a community, and the others would need to approve you joining.'

'I know. I want to stay for good. Please help me. I'm desperate.' She had started sobbing then, clearly exhausted.

There were always rooms in the cloister buildings prepared for such emergencies and Lilith had decided to settle her into one, at least until the morning. She had virtually nothing in the way of belongings but it was obvious from her clothes and speech that she was from a wealthy background. From Lilith's perspective, such members were always welcome. Summer had offered no explanation for her situation nor had Lilith asked for one. Given the distressed state she was in, it was no time for questions. They could discuss financial matters later. Just then, she had needed a hot bath, some food and sleep.

* * *

In the evenings, everyone came together in the vast refectory for dinner. It was a team effort with each resident preparing and cooking some part of it. Like the nuns before them, they grew food in the large vegetable gardens and collected fruit from the orchards. They made their own bread and crafted their own beer and wine. It was a relaxed and rewarding way of life for those who perceived it as such.

The main providers of the produce were Howard and Harriet — a middle-aged couple who had been attracted to a life that lacked dull routine and onerous responsibility. In a previous existence — because that's all it was — they had owned a small tobacco shop on Richington High Street and had lived in the flat above. It had been tolerable until tobacco became unpopular and they'd found they were working twelve-hour days but barely scraping a living. They had finally sold up to a fast-food company and joined the commune. It had been a revelation. They discovered they had a gift for growing food and the extensive convent kitchen gardens gave them free rein to exploit this new-found delight. There was even a small but deep lake, well stocked with trout, where Howard rediscovered his love of angling. They were perpetually cheerful and never tired of telling each other they should have done it long ago. They had inadvertently become parent figures to any lost souls who happened to come to the commune. Being childless themselves, this gave them added satisfaction.

'Come along, everyone, it's your favourite this evening — cottage pie and fresh vegetables.' Harriet clucked around them like a mother hen.

'I hope it's vegan,' simpered Trottie. 'I can't bear the thought of anything ripped from a poor little animal finding its way onto my plate.' She pulled a face. Trottie and her partner, Len, didn't seem to eat anything much besides lentils, kale and quinoa. They sported a variety of matching T-shirts, all of which bore countercultural symbols of rebellion and slogans wanting to ban something. They wore Jesus sandals without socks, even in cold weather. It was less of a fashion statement than a compliance with what they believed was appropriate to their image.

'I hope it bloody well *isn't* vegan,' retorted Charlie. 'I'll be picking sesame seeds out of my teeth for the rest of the night and kale makes me fart.'

'Do you really object to eating animals,' asked Georgia, innocently, 'or do you just enjoy making a fuss?' Georgia was as glamorous as her name suggested. She was also smart and well educated. Charlie wondered what she was doing here but he was glad that she was.

'Ignore 'em, lass,' said Len, in what he fondly believed was a north country working-class accent, even though he actually came from the stockbroker belt of Surrey and had been to one of the country's top public schools. 'They're nowt but symbols o' late-stage capitalism — puppets o' t' system.'

'Now, now,' chided Howard. 'No political arguments at mealtimes. You'll all get indigestion. There's a vegan option for Len and Trottie. Everyone else, tuck in.'

Lilith took Harriet to one side. 'Do you think you could coax Summer out of her room and persuade her to come down and eat something?'

'Yes, of course. The poor lamb's so thin and she's eaten nothing all day. If she doesn't want to come down, I'll take her something up on a tray.' She hurried off.

Howard and Harriet didn't contribute as much financially as some of the others, but Lilith conceded that they more than made up for it in other ways. She looked up as Gideon sidled in, unobtrusively. He was always late to dinner, scoffed his food rapidly and left immediately afterwards. He barely spoke to anyone. His donations to the Foundation were more than generous, so Lilith didn't care whether he socialized or not. He dressed as a stereotypical hippy from the seventies, albeit less colourful — long tangled hair, bushy beard and moustache, faded, bell-bottom jeans and a fringed jacket. He wore suede moccasins, regardless of the weather, and small, circular John Lennon sunglasses, even indoors. It was virtually impossible to guess his age, and in that dated get-up it was practically a disguise. Lilith reckoned even his mother would be hard pressed to recognize him. But he was inoffensive, caused no trouble and kept mainly to his room, except when he took himself off for long periods, walking in the grounds.

'Before we eat, let us join hands and chant the mantra that is the very essence of our Foundation,' said Solomon.

'Maybe Len and Trottie could give us a couple of choruses of "The Red Flag",' whispered Charlie. Georgia giggled.

Solomon gave them a withering look then began to chant, 'My spirit is free . . . my spirit is free . . .' and the twenty-odd people around the table joined in.

Mae played the flute. A generously built lady of uncertain age, she provided musical accompaniment to most group activities, whether she was asked to or not. She floated about the convent in voluminous floral dresses and a large straw hat, with flowers from the garden tucked into the brim. Her background was vague and she made no attempt to fill in the details. The most she had revealed when she joined the Foundation was that she had been a professional musician, playing with the Royal Philharmonic Orchestra, but had given it up, opting for a life on the road in a camper van with her dog, Goliath. He was a giant of an animal — a cross between an English Mastiff and a Caucasian Shepherd Dog. Weighing in at a good 200 pounds, he had a shoulder height of more than three feet. Despite his size, he was gentle and affectionate and, as Mae pointed out, he was only dangerous if he accidentally sat on you. Goliath was accepted by everyone in the commune apart from Trottie, who was terrified of him. As is often the way with dogs, he sensed her disapproval and was desperate to make friends. Whenever he saw her, he would run at her, barking joyfully, and attempt to put his massive paws on her shoulders to say hello properly. She would scream and fall over backwards, while he tried to lick her face, until a couple of the others pulled him off.

There was only one member of the commune that Goliath avoided whenever possible. For some reason, known only to a discerning dog, he regarded Solomon with suspicion. If they were in the same room, Goliath was watchful — almost vigilant. He would lie under the table and howl if Solomon approached. Mae didn't understand. Gollie loved all of humanity. It wasn't as if Solomon had ever ill-treated him; he barely even acknowledged the existence of the animal. Could it be that Goliath's 'sixth sense' detected something about Solomon that was beyond the capacity of merely five human senses? A gut feeling when something doesn't feel right? Whatever it was, Goliath's acute sense of smell and ability to read body language told him that Solomon was bad news.

CHAPTER TWO

Saturday was Detective Inspector Jack Dawes's day off and he was taking it easy. His wife, Corrie, was in town, working at her catering business — Coriander's Cuisine — and wouldn't be home until late. Saturday was her busiest day with orders and deliveries for dinner party food from the posh folk of Kings Richington, who either didn't want to cook it themselves or didn't know how. Before she left, she had given Jack instructions to clear out the garage. It was, she said, full of his junk and she needed the storage space. He had viewed it briefly — very briefly — then decided to watch the rugby instead. It was a summer test, Scotland versus France at Murrayfield and it promised to be a good match. As a young man, rugby had been Jack's passion, second only to the police service, and it accounted for his somewhat repositioned features, especially his off-centre nose.

He settled down with some cans and a pepperoni pizza that he had smuggled in from Corrie's Kitchen — a fast-food outlet run by Corrie's deputy, Carlene. It was excellent food and she did a roaring trade, particularly at weekends. He had barely bitten into a slice when the phone rang.

'Jack?' said a familiar voice. 'Sorry to bother you on your day off but you're needed here — we've got a nasty one.' It was Sergeant Mike 'Bugsy' Malone from the Murder Investigation Team.

'How nasty?' asked Jack, reluctant to abandon the match or his pizza.

'Very nasty, guv. We've got the body of a dead bloke. He's — well, he's sort of inside a tomb.'

'Don't all tombs have dead bodies in them?' asked Jack, reasonably.

'Not like this one, guv.'

'Are you sure it's a case for MIT? Mightn't he have got drunk, bashed his head and just fallen in?' Jack's pizza was starting to wilt. He took another bite.

'Doubt it. He's been disembowelled. His tripe is spread all over the ground.'

'Blimey!' Suddenly, Jack didn't fancy his pizza, smothered as it was in tomato and chunks of pepperoni sausage. 'OK, I'm on my way. Where is it?'

'In the middle of Richington Forest. You can't miss it. Uniform are all over it like a rash, wrapping tape around the trees.'

* * *

Twenty minutes later, Jack ducked under the police tape and strode towards the action. He stood for a moment, taking in the horrific scene and wondering, not for the first time, at the degree of depravity that one human being can inflict upon another — assuming it was a human being that was responsible for this bloodbath. He guessed such reflection came with age, as he couldn't remember pondering much about the philosophy of murder as a young copper.

Sergeant Malone was waiting for him with Detective Constable Aled Williams, whose face was tinged with green.

Jack stared at the carnage. He took a deep breath and was rewarded with an abattoir stench. 'Do we know who he is?' The body was naked.

'No, guv,' replied Malone. 'Uniform and SOCO are searching the area but haven't found any belongings or clothes with useful pockets that we could search for some form of ID.'

Jack rubbed his chin thoughtfully and checked out the surroundings. 'He couldn't have walked all the way from the road and into the forest naked, so the killer must have taken the clothes away with him — probably to delay identification.'

'Sarge,' began DC Williams, swallowing hard, 'do you think it was some kind of ritual sacrifice? I mean — why else would you rip out someone's insides and stuff the body half inside a tomb?'

Malone shook his head. 'I doubt it, son. I think that scenario is a bit rich, even for Kings Richington. I expect there'll be a perfectly rational explanation — but right now, I'm buggered if I know what it is.'

Jack asked the predictable question. 'Who found the body, Sergeant? No, don't tell me — a little old lady, walking her dog.'

'Got it in one,' grinned Malone. 'Except she wasn't little nor particularly old. The dog was a bloody great mastiff, attracted by the prospect of giblets for his dinner. It had to be restrained from running off with the poor devil's intestines around its neck, like a string of sausages.'

'If I had a pound for every corpse that's discovered by a dog walker . . .'

'. . . You'd be rich enough to hand in your papers,' finished Malone, knowing full well that it was something Jack would never contemplate. If he was a stick of rock, he'd have 'copper' written all the way through.

'Where is she now — this lady?'

'Uniform have taken her home, guv. They had to call a police van because the dog was too big to fit into a car. DC Williams managed to prevent the owner from throwing up and contaminating the crime scene.' Malone jerked a thumb at an approaching figure — stout and determined. 'Stand by your beds, lads, Big Ron's here.'

'Big Ron' was the nickname they had for Dr Veronica Hardacre, an indomitable and much-respected pathologist.

She was a big-boned woman, strong and muscular, with bristling black eyebrows and a moustache to match. She had little time for pompous senior officers who considered themselves more important than the due process of science and gave them short shrift, regardless of rank. MIT had learned to approach her cautiously and not ask what she termed 'damn fool questions'.

She stomped across and stared down at the body. 'Well, DI Dawes, I know you like a little drama in your work, but isn't this going a bit far? Normally, you content yourself with straightforward slaughter.' She bent over what remained of the corpse, looking closely at his face. Then she opened her bag, took out some instruments and performed various tests. Experience had shown that it was inadvisable to interrupt her during these proceedings.

Finally, when he thought it safe, Dawes asked, 'What can you tell us, Doctor?'

'Well, he's dead, Inspector. I can tell you that. The wound has jagged edges, as if it has been clawed, and there are bite marks, as though from a large animal.' She removed something with tweezers, placed it carefully in a specimen bag and held it up for them to see. 'Clumps of curly black fur, Inspector. Someone has gone to a great deal of trouble to make you think this man was killed by a wild beast.'

'Not a six-foot, man-eating poodle, then?' quipped Malone.

She regarded him, witheringly. 'I can do without your puerile humour on a Saturday afternoon, Sergeant. I should be at my yoga class, not rummaging through twenty feet of small intestine.'

'Sorry, Doc. Just trying to lighten the mood.' Malone was trying to imagine Big Ron in a tank top and yoga pants. He felt sorry for the instructor. He must be a brave bloke — nobody dared give Big Ron instructions of any sort.

'I'll know more after the post-mortem, but my initial opinion is that he was dead before someone performed the evisceration.'

'Do we have a time of death, Doctor?' asked Jack.

'Not yet.'

'Could you hazard a guess?'

Dr Hardacre stood up and brushed herself down. 'Only amateurs guess, Inspector, then they have to apologize afterwards. Post-mortem on Monday morning — eight thirty sharp.' She nodded to the mortuary attendants to take away the body, then picked up her bag and strode off.

Jack walked around the tomb — a rectangular, box-shaped structure made of limestone. The SOCOs were still searching it for anything useful. 'What is this thing, anyway?'

'It's the tomb of Saint Columbanus, sir,' replied Aled. 'According to the nuns who once lived in the convent, it contains a bone from his little finger. Precious relic, apparently.'

'What's it doing in the middle of Richington Forest? Why isn't it inside the convent cemetery with the other tombs?'

'Good question, sir.' Aled wore his smug, 'I know the answer to this' expression. It had once earned him a barrage of well-aimed missiles from fellow pupils, whenever he'd put up his hand in class. 'Saint Columbanus is the patron saint of motorcyclists.'

'Aled, son, they didn't have motorbikes in AD 615 and that's when he died, according to the inscription on this tomb,' observed Malone.

'No, Sarge, but he was a roving Irish monk who wandered up and down Europe doing missionary work. His love of the open road inspired the Church to suggest him as the patron saint of motorcyclists. His tomb is out here because they didn't think he would rest easy, cooped up inside the convent walls. The Catholic Church has a patron saint for just about everything — except fish and chips.'

'I didn't know you were a Catholic, Aled,' said Dawes.

Williams looked shocked. 'I'm not, sir, I'm Welsh Chapel — born and bred. I just Googled "Saint Columbanus".'

'It's a wonderful thing — Google,' remarked Malone. 'It's just a pity we can't Google "Who murdered this poor sod?" and get the answer. Then we could all go home and watch the rugby.'

One of the SOCO team approached Dawes. 'Inspector, I think you should look at this.'

They followed him to the edge of the clearing, almost into the trees. He pointed to the ground. 'Someone's burned a big circle into the grass, all the way around the perimeter of the clearing.'

'That's bloody peculiar,' said Malone. 'I've heard of crop circles, but why would anyone burn a circle in a forest?'

The SOCO pointed to the flattened forest floor inside the circle. 'It looks like the grass has been trampled down by a number of feet.'

'Can we get casts of the shoe prints?' asked Dawes.

''Fraid not, sir. They were bare feet.'

'Do we have photographs?'

The man nodded. 'I'll have them for you by Monday, sir.'

After a good deal of careful manoeuvring, the mortuary attendants finally managed to get all of the remains into a body bag. Some of it was draped across the top of the tomb. They removed it carefully, revealing that the top slab had been painted black, in contrast to the rest of the tomb, which was fashioned from white limestone. Chalked in the centre was a circle, enclosing a five-pointed star.

'What the hell is that?' Bugsy was uncharacteristically serious.

'I think it's what they call a pentacle, Sarge.' Aled leaned closer, the better to see. 'The five points of the star are supposed to represent the elements — fire, earth, air, water and spirit.'

'How d'you know that, son?' Young Aled was full of surprises. 'Is that part of your Celtic heritage, too?'

'No, Sarge. I had a girlfriend once who could read tarot cards. She read mine and reckoned the Five of Pentacles meant losing a lover — that was just before she dumped me.'

'Sounds like a load of bollocks to me,' declared Bugsy, in his frank, unequivocal manner.

16

Dawes wasn't so sure. 'And so it is to many people, Sergeant, but to others this kind of thing is very powerful.' He frowned. 'I don't know what went on here, but our job is to find out who the dead man is and why he ended up like this.'

CHAPTER THREE

It was seven o'clock on Monday morning. Despite the unpopular hour, the MIT incident room was packed. This was a particularly horrific murder with sinister connotations, and all members of the team wanted to be involved in catching the perpetrator. Sergeant Parsloe from Uniform and several of his constables had come in, always appreciated for their collective local knowledge. The whiteboard bore gruesome photographs of the crime scene and detailed pictures of the victim — as yet without an identity.

DI Dawes stood at the front. 'OK, team, let's brainstorm. What do we think we have, here? Just shout out your thoughts.'

'It's a jealousy killing, sir,' shouted a keen young PC from the back. 'The dead bloke had an assignation with another bloke's wife. They were both naked and having it away on top of the tomb — kinky, like — when her husband turned up. She grabbed her clothes and legged it while the husband separated the dead bloke from his innards with a machete, just as a warning not to do it again.'

Dawes smiled. 'Possible, Constable, if a little colourful. Anyone else?'

'Gang warfare, sir. Rival drug barons, battling it out for the territory. They took his clothes away so it would be difficult to identify him, giving them time to get back to their manor. They cut him up as an example to anyone else trying a takeover bid.'

'I reckon he's a Russian spy. The "secret squirrels" — sorry, sir, I mean the officers from Security Intelligence — tracked him to Kings Richington and eliminated him before he could poison anyone. His clothes were taken away to test for Novichok. They intended to send a quarantine van for his body but it was discovered by the dog walker before they got there.'

'All right, so what tore out his insides?' asked someone.

'Erm . . . foxes? Rats? Crows? Wildlife isn't all cute little baby rabbits, it's — well — it's wild, innit?'

'Nah, I don't think it was any of that. It was the Beast of Richington Forest, sir. There have been several recent sightings, reported by members of the public, and they weren't all nutters. If you look closely at the photograph, you can see ragged claw marks around the wound. The beast cornered him, pinned him against the tomb and ripped out his guts.' This hypothesis was accompanied by much theatrical gesturing.

'OK, smart-arse.' The young lady police constable sitting next to him ducked under his flailing arms. 'What did this beast do with his clothes? Eat them?'

The constable looked peeved. 'I never said I had all the answers, did I? The inspector wanted us to brainstorm.'

'Pity you haven't got one then,' she muttered. 'If brains were taxable, you'd get a rebate.'

Jack smiled to himself. They were a bright, imaginative lot and very keen, despite an occasional tendency to wander off into la-la land. On the whole, he reckoned the future of law and order was in safe hands, in this part of the country at least. He pointed to the photographs, pinned to the board. 'What about this symbol, chalked on top of the tomb? What's that all about?'

'Don't tramps chalk symbols on things, as a message to other tramps?' asked someone.

'They used to, once upon a time,' agreed DS Parsloe, mournfully. 'There aren't many "kings of the road" left, these days. Now, they sit on the pavement outside Sainsbury's with a dog and a cardboard placard.'

DC Gemma Fox had been quiet until now. 'I think it's something much more sinister. Aled says the symbol is a pentacle. The star inside the circle is inverted. In that form, it's a device used by Satanists for invoking the devil.'

This was received by jeering from her colleagues and accusations of 'watching too many horror films late at night.

Jack was about to ask what they made of the perimeter circle burned into the grass and the trampling of bare feet, when the door opened and Detective Chief Superintendent George Garwood strode in. Garwood was Jack's boss and a career copper, keen to avoid anything that might show him in a bad light and affect his next promotion. He liked to keep his eye on the ball, although much of the time, he didn't even know what game they were playing, never mind who had the ball.

'Inspector Dawes, I need to speak to you about the monthly returns . . .' He stopped abruptly, staring at the photographs on the whiteboard. For a moment, he seemed unable to speak, then: 'In God's name, Dawes, whatever happened here?'

'That's what we're trying to find out, sir. This man's body was found in Richington Forest, lying on a tomb. He'd been badly mutilated, as you can see. He was naked, so we have no clues to his identity and he doesn't fit any of the missing persons reports. We ran his fingerprints and DNA through the database but there wasn't a match. I'm hoping dental records might throw something up, but—'

'I know who he is,' declared Garwood, shocked. 'It's Sir Bixby Carrington. I've known him for years. How did he come to be . . . I mean — what was he . . . ?'

The incident room had suddenly gone very quiet. This was a surprise — the anonymous corpse turning out to be a mate of the old man. They waited in silence to see what else he was going to say.

'Sir, might I suggest we discuss this in your office?' advised Jack. 'I'd be grateful for any light you could shed on this investigation.' He didn't know what further disclosures there might be and felt instinctively that it was probably best if they were kept on a need-to-know basis — just until they knew what they were dealing with.

Garwood looked pale. 'Er — yes, as you wish, Jack.'

Once in his office, Garwood took out a bottle of single malt and two glasses. He poured himself a large double and offered to pour one for Jack, who shook his head, sensing that this was no time for a befuddled brain. 'How do you know Sir Bixby, sir?'

'We go back a long way. We were at university together. I entered the police service and Bixby opted for politics, like his father. All went well for him, to start with. He married Jennifer about the same time that I married Mrs Garwood and the four of us used to have dinner together and meet for the theatre. He received a knighthood for services to the government, and it seemed to the rest of us that he had achieved the perfect life.' Garwood paused and took a gulp of whisky. 'Then it all seemed to fall apart. He started drinking to excess, gambling heavily, and he stopped coming to Lodge meetings. There were rumours of other women. Finally, Jenny decided she'd had enough and she left him, taking the children with her. After that, he went from bad to worse, and Cynthia and I lost track of the Carringtons altogether. That picture on your board is the first I've seen of him in years. It was quite a shock, I can tell you.'

'Do you have any idea what it was that made Sir Bixby go off the rails?'

Garwood shook his head. 'Not a clue. It was a mystery to everyone that knew him. It was so out of character.'

'And you wouldn't have any idea what he was doing naked in Richington Forest?'

'It pains me even to speculate, Dawes. It certainly isn't the behaviour of the man I knew as a friend.'

'Well, thank you for that, sir. Now that we have an identity, we know where to start digging.' He hesitated. 'Of course, we'll have to trace Lady Carrington to inform her of the death of her husband and ask her for a formal identification.'

Garwood took another swig of whisky. 'Yes, of course. Be as sensitive as you can. Jennifer took a lot of grief from Bixby when he was alive — I'm not sure how much grief she'll feel now that he's dead. Keep me informed, will you, Dawes?'

'Of course, I will, sir.' It was the first time Jack had seen the old man anything other than his usual pompous, blustering self. He felt sorry for him.

* * *

The post-mortem had begun by the time Dawes arrived. Sergeant Malone and DC Williams were already there, suitably gowned.

Dr Hardacre glanced up as Jack came in. 'Good of you to join us, Inspector. I hope we haven't interrupted anything important, like your coffee break.'

Obviously, Bugsy and Aled hadn't told Dr Hardacre about Garwood's revelation, which would have explained why he was late. He was glad. They had recognized that it was necessary to be discreet, until they had a better fix on what had happened. He wondered how difficult it would be to find Lady Carrington.

'I'm sorry, Doctor. Have I missed anything?'

'You haven't missed the most important thing — the cause of death. His liver was shot from alcohol abuse and no doubt that would have seen him off eventually, but that wasn't what killed him, nor was it the evisceration.'

'I remember you saying, at the scene, that he had been dead before his guts spilled out,' said Malone.

'Correct, Sergeant. Our friend here died between midnight on Friday and four o'clock the following morning. Cause of death was hypoxemia and cerebral anoxia due to prolonged submersion in water.'

'He drowned?' chorused Bugsy and Aled, who hadn't seen that coming.

'In my expert opinion, yes, he did. There were traces of froth in his airways and water in what remained of his stomach. The only signs of violence are the claw and bite marks, which — again, in my opinion — were inflicted after death and nothing to do with the cause of it.'

'Could the drowning have been accidental?' questioned Dawes. 'There's no evidence of him being knocked out or bruises from being held under.'

She pursed her lips, causing her moustache to pucker. 'Possibly. On the other hand, he had enough alcohol and lysergic acid diethylamide —that's LSD to you, Inspector — in his system to space out an elephant. In that state, he'd have been absolutely suggestible and without the ability to reason. He could quite easily have fallen into water or been pushed into it, without even noticing the difference. As I mentioned, the evisceration definitely took place after he was pulled out.'

'What about the clumps of dog fur, Doc?' Malone asked.

'Might they have belonged to the dog that found the body?' asked Dawes. 'Apparently it had a good snuffle around in the entrails before the owner could restrain it.'

She shook her head. 'No — for two reasons. Firstly, the dog that found the body was mostly English Mastiff, apricot-fawn coloured, with a short, close-lying coat. Entirely the wrong type. And secondly, it isn't dog fur. The laboratory had quite a task deciding what animal it belonged to because it was quite rare. The closest they could get was that it's the secondary, curly hair from an Angora goat, possibly a Belgian breed. It started off white but had been dyed black for some obscure reason. I concede that the saliva I found around the teeth marks belonged to a dog — probably the mastiff — but it definitely did not tear out the poor man's insides. That was done with a sharp, claw-like tool, possibly an old farm implement. If you could find it, Inspector Dawes, I could try to match it to the wounds.'

'But why would anyone do that to a dead body?' asked Dawes. 'It isn't as if they wanted to conceal his identity — his face is unmarked.'

She shrugged. 'I think that one's down to you, Inspector. I only do the "how" and the "when". The "why" is your job.'

'How can you drown in a forest?' asked Aled, becoming more puzzled with every revelation. 'I suppose he could have drowned in a quiet bit of the Thames, but then his body would have to have been transported somehow to where we found it. You can't drive a car right up to that clearing from the road.'

'This may help you find the location.' Dr Hardacre stretched out a hand to Miss Catwater, her assistant. 'Marigold — the *Potamogetonaceae*, if you please.' Miss Catwater rarely spoke during a post-mortem but knew instinctively what was required at any time. She placed a kidney dish in the doctor's hand. Big Ron held it out to the police officers. They peered at what looked like green slime. 'Pondweed, gentlemen. The deceased drowned in a lake — and one inhabited by *Oncorhynchus mykiss*, if I'm not much mistaken. I found some scales in his hair. There was also a *Nymphaeaceae* petal. You're looking for a small but deep body of water with water lilies and stocked with rainbow trout.'

'Any thoughts on the significance of the pentacle chalked on the tomb, Doc?' asked Malone.

'I'm a pathologist, Sergeant, not a fortune teller. If you're looking for that kind of nonsense, you could try Professor MacDuff. He's a professor of demonology — mad as a box of frogs, of course. Good day, gentlemen.'

CHAPTER FOUR

Charlie Updike kick-started the Harley, flung it into gear, and roared off down the track. It took him past the chapel, past the priest's house and out into open parkland. It was good to feel the wind in his hair, with no requirement for a helmet as long as he stayed within the twelve-foot wall that formed the convent boundary. The atmosphere within the Foundation of the Free Spirit was, in his view, far from free — more like claustrophobic. What with Solomon strutting around like a tinpot dictator and Urbain chasing skirt all day, only Lilith seemed to have any business sense. And that's what this place was, when you came right down to it: a business, and a pretty lucrative one from what he could see.

Before he came here, Charlie thought he'd had some knowledge of what it was like to live in an institution, but he had little real concept of life inside a cult. He was twenty-five years old, good looking in a raffish sort of way and ready to take on the world — if that's what it took to get where he wanted to be. He'd arrived with the idea that there *is* no cult without a powerful, charismatic leader with the uncanny ability to get susceptible people to follow him unquestioningly. Cult members are devoted to the leader, not to the leader's ideas. He therefore has total control over his followers — there is no questioning his decisions and he is accountable to no one. Charlie had researched the many precedents to this model of a cult leader, and in his view, Solomon couldn't lead a conga line.

Old Howie and his missus were the good guys. They seemed happy with their lot and didn't look for anything more. Len and Trottie were obviously fake — armchair socialists of the worst kind. It was one thing to be a committed 'leftie', but to pretend was just a betrayal of the people who seemed to take it seriously. Charlie didn't know what to make of Gideon. His hands shook badly. Charlie wondered if it was due to alcohol or too much caffeine. There was a backstory there, he was convinced. Worth keeping an eye on, anyway. He hadn't seen much of the new kid — Summer. Probably a case of falling out with Mum and Dad and they'd turn up to fetch her in a day or two. Tearful reconciliation and goodbye Summer. Mae and Goliath were like a wrestling tag team. The dog clearly adored her and regularly showed it by tussling her to the ground and licking her. Not when she was playing her flute, though. It seemed to hypnotize him into a state of calm. It had a similar effect on some of the members. Charlie wasn't a fan of classical music — he was more into heavy metal — but somehow the sound of Mae's flute seemed appropriate to the surroundings. Atmospheric, even. But what circumstances, he wondered, had caused a professional musician to give up the RPO and travel about the country in a camper van?

Now, Georgia really was an enigma — intelligent, funny, a real looker and nobody's fool. He'd spent more time getting to know her than any of them, much to Urbain's annoyance. He could have told him, *You're wasting your time, mate, she isn't interested.* He thought he might take her for a ride on the back of his bike when she wasn't studying on her laptop. He'd tried to look over her shoulder to see what it was that she found so important, but she always closed it before he could read anything. As for the rest of the cult, they did a lot of chanting and dancing around, holding hands and picking flowers, but nothing of interest to him. There was a Hindu chap — Rushil — who came and went, mostly floating silently about the grounds in a long white tunic. He held yoga classes on the lawn, which were well attended. Charlie thought he seemed a nice enough bloke and he was very good looking, according to Georgia.

He'd reached a small hut that stood at the far end of the convent estate, close to the lake. It was full of old gardening tools and a creaky wheelbarrow. The gardening nuns must have used it as storage. He heaved the bike up onto its stand and went inside. In the corner, there was a small cupboard that housed flower pots, gardening gloves and slug pellets. He opened it and pulled out his mobile phone, hidden inside one of the gloves. Phones were confiscated when you joined the cult. Solomon said they were a distraction from meditation and contrary to the aims of the Foundation, which included total partition from the banal trivialities of the outside world. Charlie had a portable phone charger that he kept topped up from the socket in his room. He plugged it into his phone and punched in a speed dial.

'Hello? Yes, it's me — Charlie. Is the boss there? There's been a development.'

* * *

News of the disembowelled body, found on a tomb in the forest, reached the *Richington Echo* at the speed of light, and the editor plastered it all over the front page of the early edition. Inevitably, emails to the editor came thick and fast, propounding all manner of bizarre theories. The most popular was that it was the work of the Beast of Richington Forest. It seemed that everybody loved a good 'beast' legend, and accounts varied from a massive black panther to a Baskerville-type hound, walking on its hind legs. Actual descriptions were vague as it had only ever been 'seen' at night, in the dark, and it hadn't hung around long enough to be photographed on anyone's phone. In the absence of any photographs of the corpse, which the editor would really have liked, he contented himself with library pictures of a snarling panther with glowing eyes and slavering jaws.

Jack went to see the desk sergeant who had filled out the report forms mentioned at the briefing. He was a long-serving officer with no illusions about the tendency for some members of the public to 'lay it on thick', to say the least.

'I've heard it all, Inspector. Once a rumour starts, it's crackpot alert. I get them in here with tales of werewolves with fangs, vampires in black capes and animals that can shape-shift and disappear in a puff of smoke. One lady reckoned she saw a 'big black thing with horns'. It doesn't help that most of 'em use the forest as a shortcut home from the Richington Arms, after too much booze. But I'm convinced that one or two of the serious witnesses have seen *something*. I'm not suggesting it's a wild beast, but their accounts tally — a glimpse of curly black fur and an unpleasant, rotting smell, as it rustles through the trees.'

Unfortunately, the editor of the *Echo* had taken his usual stance and printed the most sensational versions, criticizing the police for not taking action before someone else was attacked and killed by this 'monster'. Why weren't they staking out the forest at night? Were they afraid the 'beast' would devour them? How long before they identified the victim? Had his next of kin been informed, and if not, why not?

That, at least, was a fair question, thought Jack. They had to find Lady Carrington before Sir Bixby's identity was leaked to the press, as these things invariably were. As it turned out, Chief Superintendent Garwood's wife, Cynthia, was able to help.

* * *

When George arrived home, Cynthia could tell from his face that he was upset. He was always in a strop about something that had gone wrong at the station — he was that kind of man and she was used to it — but she sensed that this was something more. She left him in peace until he'd changed and settled in his chair, then she poured them both a large gin and tonic, although it was rather early.

'George, is everything all right, dear?'

Wordlessly, he passed her a copy of the *Echo* with its sensationalist headlines. She read it twice. 'Georgie, this is awful. That poor man, abandoned in the forest with his insides torn out. Do the police know who he is?'

'I do — I recognized him from the ghastly photographs in the incident room, and now, Jack Dawes knows, too.' He pinched the bridge of his nose where a headache was starting. 'Cynthia — it's Bixby.'

She took an involuntary breath. 'Not Bixby Carrington? My God, I knew he'd gone a bit wrong but not this! Poor Jennifer. Does she know?'

'Not yet. We haven't been able to trace her. I think she may have gone abroad after she left Bixby.'

Cynthia jumped up. 'No, she didn't. She changed her name and went to live in John o'Groats. She sent us a Christmas card, don't you remember?' She went to a drawer and fished it out. 'Look, she's written her address on the back. She moved to Scotland with the two children. She said she wanted to get as far away from Bixby as she could.'

'She managed that, all right. It's about 700 miles.' Garwood looked at the card. 'I don't remember seeing this, but then I leave birthdays, Christmas and such to you. You're so much better at the social niceties.'

Cynthia reckoned that excuse was used by most husbands to avoid what they saw as unnecessary feminine fuss. 'What will you do — ask the Scottish Police to tell her about Bixby?'

George pondered. 'Yes, initially. But Bixby and I were good friends, years ago. I was his best man. I think I owe it to him to explain personally to Jennifer the circumstances surrounding his death.'

Cynthia read the lurid news article again. 'You won't tell her he was savaged by a wild beast?'

'No, of course not. I don't believe for one moment that he was. The pathology report said it was death by drowning. It also said his system was full of alcohol and a hallucinogenic drug. I shan't tell her that, either.'

'If he drowned, why was his body ripped open, like it says here?'

'We don't know, yet. I've got Dawes on the case — I've no doubt he'll get to the bottom of it.'

CHAPTER FIVE

Corrie Dawes was grilling gammon steaks to go with fresh pineapple and a nice crisp salad for supper. She'd been working at Coriander's Cuisine all day, and tonight, Carlene, her deputy, was cooking at Chez Carlene — yet another arm of the catering business. The bistro, to Carlene's joy and utter amazement, had recently been awarded a Michelin star. It was always busy and had a great reputation for classic French food at a reasonable price.

Corrie looked at the clock — Jack was late, as she expected. The story of the Beast of Richington Forest had gone viral, and several of her customers had asked if her husband was any closer to catching it. She had been tempted to reply that he was out there now with a big net and a pointed stick, but sarcasm wasn't the way to keep good customers, and it would have gone right over the heads of the ones who were daft enough to ask. She heard his key in the door.

'What's for supper? I'm starving.' He looked at the meal she was dishing up. 'No chips? You can't have gammon without chips and a fried egg.'

'Have you looked at your tummy recently? You won't pass your next police fitness test if we don't get you a bit slimmer.'

'Nonsense, I can do the fifteen-metre shuttle run with-out any problems.' He held his stomach in and did some running on the spot. 'Look at that. Nothing wrong with my legs.' There was crack like a pistol shot from one of his knees. He grimaced and limped to a chair.

'Why don't you do a bit of road work with Bugsy, like you did last year?' suggested Corrie. Jack still hadn't fully recovered from the sight of his portly sergeant in running gear. There were rotating neutron stars in the galaxy less conspicuous than Bugsy in silver spandex.

'He isn't doing it any more. He argued that he came into this world with a bald head and fat stomach so he might as well leave in the same condition.'

'You'd better be able to run a bit sharpish if the "beast" comes after you,' she joked.

He massaged his knee. 'Don't you start. There is no beast. People just like scaremongering. The poor devil drowned and I'm not surprised — he was full of drink and drugs.'

'It said in the *Echo* that you haven't identified him yet. You'd think someone would have reported him missing by now.'

'He hasn't been formally identified, but he was an old mate of George's. He doesn't want it made public until the widow has been told.'

'Is that going to be down to you and Bugsy?'

'No, she moved back to Scotland after they split up so the local police are going to do the "death call". The old man's flying up there tomorrow to fill in the details. He wants all this "beast" nonsense discredited by the time he comes back. He doesn't want her to think her husband was devoured by a wild beast due to police negligence.'

'That's all very well but now the press has got hold of it, people are looking for a proper explanation — something with substance.'

'I know how they feel.' Jack picked up his knife and fork. 'I suppose a baked potato is out of the question.'

* * *

After a longish flight and an even longer journey from the airport at Wick, George Garwood found Jennifer running a tea shop in a village near John o'Groats, where she had been born and brought up. She had dropped the name and title Lady Carrington when she split with Bixby and had reverted to her maiden name. Now she was simply Jenny Mackenzie of the Lochside Tea Shop. Their son and daughter were grown up and had left home — first for university and then to pursue successful careers of their own.

Jennifer greeted George warmly, as if the friends had last met only yesterday. 'Thank you for coming all this way, George.'

He kissed her on both cheeks. She had put on weight since he last saw her and her hair was starting to grey a little, but she looked much less stressed and unhappy. He was glad. Even though Bixby had been his great friend, he had to acknowledge that he had treated his wife badly. 'I'm just so sorry it had to be in such sad circumstances.'

She smiled. 'To be honest, it wasn't a surprise when the local police came to see me with the news about Bixby. It was always going to end badly for him. They said that you would give me more details about how he died when you arrived.' She had closed the tea shop and took George through to her small flat at the back.

'I only wish I had all the information, Jenny. My team are working on it as we speak. All I can tell you for certain is that Bixby died from drowning.' He saw no reason to distress her with the — literally — gory details.

She looked shocked. 'But he was an excellent swimmer — even as a young man. How could that possibly have happened?' She paused. 'I know what you're not telling me, George. He was drunk, wasn't he? It's kind of you to try to spare me, but I had no illusions about the man I married. And to whom I am still married. We never bothered with divorce.'

If only that were the worst of it, thought Garwood. 'I'm afraid the pathologist did find a considerable amount of alcohol in his system at the post-mortem. Until we know more, we have to assume he fell into the water while under the influence and couldn't get out.'

'Was there no one to help him?' she asked.

Garwood hesitated, grateful that the circulation of the *Richington Echo* did not extend as far as Scotland. 'No, it happened during the night. His body was discovered early the next day.'

'Did somebody find him floating in the water and pull him out?'

'Something like that,' he lied. To date, Dawes and his team had no clue as to how Carrington had come to be on the tomb without his clothes and with what appeared to be serious evidence of an animal attack, despite Dr Hardacre's advice to the contrary. 'Have you had any recent contact with Bixby?'

She was reluctant for a moment. 'A little. He sent me a text message about a week ago asking for money. Naturally, I didn't give him any. My husband had what I believe is described as an addictive personality. He drank far too much, gambled heavily, and there were women — I always knew that. But recently, it had got worse. He appeared to be caught up in something that was out of control. He was scared, he said, but he didn't know how to stop it. Find out, George, in case there are others in the same trouble.'

In view of the distance, it had been arranged that as a secondary identification to the one Garwood had provided, Jennifer could be shown pictures — suitably censored — online. She was sad but not grief stricken.

'Poor Bixby. He's finally at peace now. I think he had been battling with his inner demons for some time. Now they can't torment him any longer.' She hesitated, wondering whether to ask. 'George, I don't suppose you found his watch? I only ask because it has sentimental value. I bought it for him in happier days, as an anniversary present. It's engraved and worth quite a lot of money.'

Garwood cast his mind back to the photograph of Carrington's body — an image he'd been trying hard to forget. There had been no watch on his wrist, but he wasn't about to tell her that George had been naked and ripped apart. 'I'm sorry, Jenny, we didn't find a watch.'

She shrugged. 'I expect he pawned it to pay his gambling debts.'

* * *

George returned home tired and dejected. It had been a sad visit but it had brought back memories of cheerier times, more years ago than he cared to remember. Now, an old friend was dead and his widow was relying on George to find out how and why. He had rarely felt the weight of his job as much as he did right now. He was glad DI Dawes was on the case. Despite the feelings of inferiority that Dawes always seemed to generate in him, Garwood knew there was no better man for the job.

Cynthia thought her husband deserved a decent dinner, so she ordered a meal from Coriander's Cuisine. She and Corrie had been at school together and had become good friends over the years. It wasn't unknown for them to get involved in dangerous situations that their husbands would prefer them to have avoided. Corrie delivered the food personally, while George was taking a hot bath with a large glass of the single malt whisky that Jenny had given him as a thank you for travelling such a long way to see her.

'Dreadful business,' said Corrie, arranging the crown of lamb — George's favourite — on a serving dish.

'I know,' agreed Cynthia. She wondered, not for the first time, how Corrie managed to produce amazing meals with no apparent effort. 'Poor Jenny was so sad and she doesn't know the half of it.'

Corrie turned out the summer pudding — another of George's favourites. 'You don't think there's any truth in the rumours about a wild beast on the loose, do you? Jack says it's nonsense.'

'So does George. But you can't help wondering. I mean, something must have torn out Bixby's insides. Apparently, several members of the public have reported seeing a large animal loose in the forest. They can't all have been pissed.'

Corrie nodded. 'I agree. But Jack and George are career coppers. They're hung up on the policeman's holy trinity — means, motive and opportunity. Sometimes you have to think outside the box.'

* * *

It was on the subject of 'thinking outside the box' that Jack and Bugsy decided to follow Big Ron's suggestion and visit Professor MacDuff. To date, no one had come up with a credible explanation for the circle burned into the clearing in Richington Forest, nor the significance of the pentacle chalked on the tomb. They were no closer to finding out who had left the eviscerated corpse there and, as Bugsy pointed out, if the old boy was indeed 'mad as a box of frogs' they could just make their excuses and leave.

'People need belief systems, gentlemen.' The professor was delighted to offer the police the benefit of his years of research into what he believed was a fascinating and important subject. 'That's what demonology is — a belief system with just the same licence as Christianity.' He picked up a heavy, cut-glass decanter. 'I usually take a wee dram about now. Can I interest you . . . ?'

Jack and Bugsy declined. When he poured the whisky into a glass, Bugsy half expected green vapour to rise. Then he reminded himself that the professor wasn't a wizard doing magic tricks but a bona fide expert on his subject.

'What is it I can help you with?' asked MacDuff.

Jack began tentatively, wondering what he was doing here, discussing devils.

'Is there any substance to the belief in demons, among modern academics, Professor? I mean, isn't it simply the stuff of horror films and paperbacks?'

'Och, no! The literature of demonology produced between the fifteenth and eighteenth centuries influenced the intellectual and cultural history of late medieval and early modern Europe. It's no longer regarded as merely incidental — it's been integrated into an entire dimension of thought.'

'I think I'm losing you, Prof,' said Bugsy.

'Sorry, Sergeant Malone. Let me put it another way. Human nature is generally believed to be innately weak, sinful and vulnerable to demonic temptation. We are able to distinguish right from wrong, but we might not always choose right, for a number of reasons. For example, servants of the devil could, either on their own or with the devil acting through them, harm or illicitly influence other people by occult. Flawed perceptions and flexible wills allow them to be led astray.'

'What you're saying is that people may commit crimes, believing they are being influenced by the devil,' said Jack.

'Precisely, Inspector.'

'Or they may be doing something they know is wrong but using the devil as an excuse.' Bugsy wasn't convinced.

'Sergeant, if you ask someone if they believe in demons, there are usually three answers: "*Yes, of course I do. I battle with mine every day.*" "*No, of course not. Silly question.*" Or, "*I'm not sure. Like ghosts, there are more things in heaven and earth than we fully understand.*" Their perspective would give you some idea of whether they are culpable of whatever crime you suspect them to have committed.'

Bugsy pulled a piece of paper from his pocket, on which he had drawn the circle containing a star that was chalked on the tomb. He smoothed it out and put it before the professor. 'What's this, Prof?'

MacDuff looked at it and frowned. 'That's the Sigil of Baphomet, a symbol for the Horned God. With the point of the star facing down, it represents carnality and earthly wickedness. Satanists use it as a sign of rebellion and to reject the symbol of the Holy Trinity.'

'Blimey!' muttered Bugsy. He and Jack exchanged bemused glances.

The professor continued. 'Each point of the star is related to the elements — the demons of the air, the phantoms of water, the devils of fire, the ghosts of the earth and, enchaining them all, the evil of the spirit. It's seen by some as a manifestation tool. By that, I mean the star acts as a portal for demons while the circle contains them — protecting the summoner and allowing the demons to remain within our human plane for longer. Where have you seen this, Sergeant?'

Bugsy looked at Jack, who nodded approval. 'It was chalked on a tomb under a body that had been eviscerated.'

'Och, dear me.' The professor looked worried. 'I'm afraid that's nae good — nae good at all. You must take great care with your investigation. There are surely dark forces at work here.'

Back in the car, Bugsy said, 'What did you make of that?'

'I'm not sure. I think what the old boy was trying to tell us is that demons can take many forms, some of them human.'

'Well, if I decide to sell my soul to a demon, I'll summon more than one — to push up the bidding,' said Bugsy, pragmatic as ever and totally unaffected by threats of the supernatural. He opened the glove compartment and took out a greasy paper bag. 'D'you fancy a doughnut?'

CHAPTER SIX

'We can't afford any more mistakes,' declared Lilith, firmly. She had called Solomon and Urbain to a 'meeting of minds' in the Lodge — a private part of the commune estate, now used as a staffroom. In the days of St Columbanus's convent, it was reserved for the priest, nuns having been forbidden to go there. Cult members were now similarly discouraged by large 'No Entry' signs on the gate, but for different reasons than the nuns.

'I should like to point out that I haven't made any mistakes.' Solomon had a hubristic belief in his own self-proclaimed genius. 'What happened was due to the intervention of a power far higher than mine — a power that has the ability, through ritual, to focus thought and energy into deeds. I don't expect you to understand.'

'Don't be an arse, Sol,' scoffed Urbain. 'We know what happened and it had nothing to do with your pantomime act.'

Solomon leaped to his feet, incensed. 'How dare you! I am a portal — a bona fide summoner of the supreme hierarchy!' He grasped the pentacle on the chain around his neck in much the same way that shocked old ladies clutch at their pearls. 'You have no idea of the stress it places on my body and my fragile nervous system. It's no joke leaping onto that tomb with my rheumatism, never mind sitting cross-legged on a slab of stone for an hour. I suffer pain and personal sacrifice—'

'And piles,' laughed Urbain. 'I've seen the ointment in your medicine cabinet. And if I were you, I'd take a look at those curly, goat-hair tights you wear. They're starting to moult. They look indecently threadbare in places. It's a good job all your performances are at night, by candlelight. If your "disciples" ever see you in daylight, you won't get many volunteers for the initiation ceremony. Speaking of which, I've often wondered, Sol, when you get to the part where you have to shag the "virgin", how do you pull it out of those tight leggings? Have they got a fly, like trousers?'

Solomon made to leave. 'I don't have to put up with this. My role isn't some sort of comedy act to be ridiculed. I don't know why I waste my talents on barbarians like you.'

'Because you want your share of the loot, like the rest of us.'

Lilith ignored the contretemps and continued with the business in hand. 'Have you put the message in the personal column of the *Echo*, Solomon?'

He sat down again. 'No. Astaroth has not yet commanded it.'

'Well, he'd better make his mind up soon or we'll lose our regulars.'

'I think we should do more to attract younger devotees,' suggested Urbain. He examined his fingernails, which he always kept professionally manicured, though today were looking rather ragged. He made a mental note to make an appointment with that young manicurist in town.

Lilith frowned. 'Try to stay focused on the main purpose of the Foundation, Urbain. It isn't to provide you with a constant supply of young women.'

He grinned. 'How very unkind. I'll have you know that without me, this place would have no spiritual ethos at all. I provide the aesthetics, the appreciation of beauty and artistic taste — and it isn't easy, with some of the dross I have to work with.'

'Has Rushil's next yoga class been advertised in the newspaper?' asked Solomon. 'It's imperative that we avoid any misunderstanding. Astaroth is most powerful on Fridays between the eleventh hour and midnight. Rushil's yoga classes are between eleven and noon on Fridays. We don't want people to arrive expecting Astaroth's glorious celebration, only to be greeted by Rushil's "Namaste" and a request to assume the downward dog position.'

Lilith patted his arm. 'Stop worrying, little brother, I have everything under control. If we each stick to what we're good at, there won't be any more trouble.'

* * *

Len and Trottie waited until the other members of the Foundation had settled down for the night and all was quiet. It was ten o'clock when they sneaked out of the commune house with their torches and crept as silently as possible down the track to the row of buildings furthest away from the main convent.

'This was a spiffing idea of mine, the location is perfect,' said Len, whose real name was Tristan and was no longer bothering to speak in his fake, flat-cap accent.

'I think you'll find that it was I who found it,' objected Trottie — alias Millicent.

'Millie, dear heart, I don't think you did. We were on holibobs in Zurich when I spotted that dear little convent, halfway up a mountain, and I said, "A convent would be utterly the best place for our business." Don't you remember?'

She pulled a petulant face. 'Well, all right, but I thought up our names.' They both chuckled. 'Do you suppose any of those bourgeois peeps realize we call ourselves after Lenin and Trotsky?'

'Not a chance. They wouldn't know a champagne socialist from a banana daiquiri. It was *ingenious* of us to pretend to be loony lefties, rebelling against the establishment. After we've gone, if anyone's asked by the cops to describe us, they'll say we had northern accents, wore scruffy T-shirts with communist slogans and had no manners.'

'And that we were vegans. Don't forget that, Tris. I shouldn't want to think I've been eating all that disgusting food for nothing.'

They stopped outside the last building, set back from the lane. It was the largest in the row, originally set aside by the nuns for storing the food and wine that the convent produced, then sold for a meagre income. Its current use, however, was designed to produce an income that would be considerably more than meagre. The windows were boarded up but Tristan had reconnected the water and electricity. He unlocked the sturdy padlock and they went inside, quickly closing the door behind them. For a few moments, they proudly surveyed the sea of green and the expensive set-up supporting it — LED lights, climate control equipment, and an air-flow fan with a charcoal filter, to minimize any telltale odour.

'Isn't that the most beautiful thing you've ever seen?' enthused Tristan.

'Simply fabulosa, darling,' agreed Millie.

'Come on, let's get started. We don't have long.'

When they had finished their work, they replaced the padlock and Tristan checked to make sure no light could be seen from outside. 'Are you hungry, Mills?'

'Absolutely starvingtons, sweetie. If I have to eat any more of Harriet's ghastly kale in coconut milk, it'll be upchuck city.'

He looked at his watch. 'That bistro in town is still open. I believe it's called Chez Carlene. It has a Michelin star — shall we try it out? I could murder a steak and chips.'

'Ooh yah, me too. Totes delish! This vegan thing is good for the poor little animals and all that, but the food is totally pukesville.'

As they made their way back to the commune, a dark figure emerged, unseen, from the shadows and watched them go. Gideon was taking one of his nightly walks. Plagued with nightmares, his insomnia was little better than it had been when he'd first arrived. No matter what method he used to calm his mind — and he'd tried them all — he couldn't rid himself of the smell of blood, the lifeless body on the table, the feeling of sheer failure and guilt. His hands shook pretty much all of the time. Briefly, he wondered where the two lefties were going. They were a joke, in his view, but this wasn't a prison, the gates weren't locked, and while he doubted that Lilith would approve of cult members leaving the house on any pretext, especially late at night, it had nothing to do with him. He had his own demons to fight.

* * *

Georgia had been with the Foundation of the Free Spirit for a month. Before she came, she'd had no preconceived ideas of how or why people lived within a cult. For her purposes, it was better to keep an open mind. She had since gained the impression that some of the others — the ones who chanted mantras and planted willow twigs as a gift to the fairies — had such open minds that their brains had fallen out.

She was vigilant but not so overtly as to arouse suspicion. Certainly, she had detected an underlying atmosphere to what was supposed to be a carefree existence. Nothing she had been able to put a finger on, but it was there nonetheless. Her mission was to stay for as long as it took to find out what had actually happened and why. It was late by the time she had completed the notes on her laptop and she realized she was ravenous. She was just contemplating a raid on the kitchen when there was a tap on her door.

'It's open. Who is it?'

Seeing her light on, Charlie had thought it was worth putting his head around the door and chancing his arm — a complicated manoeuvre, not without risk. 'It's me — your friendly neighbourhood biker. I was just thinking about going for a burn into Richington and back. Thought you might like to come.'

'Only if you're going to buy me supper. I haven't eaten since breakfast and that was only one of Len and Trottie's chewy granola bars.'

Charlie couldn't believe his luck. He'd been sure she'd tell him to shove off. 'Absolutely — is anywhere open at this time of night?'

'Yep. There's a bistro called Chez Carlene. Open for orders until midnight and often later, so I believe.'

'Right, let's go. I have a spare helmet.'

* * *

Despite the hour, Chez Carlene was 'rammed', as Carlene herself would have put it. She ran it with her French boyfriend, Antoine, and there was nothing they liked better than to see customers relaxing to Left Bank accordion music and enjoying the food and wine. Following the award of the Michelin star, business had boomed, pulling in customers from all around the Thames catchment area. They'd had to take on a sous-chef and an additional waiter to cope with the extra customers.

Charlie and Georgia were shown to a recently vacated table in the window and had just ordered when a taxi pulled up outside. Georgia nudged Charlie. 'Look who's just come in.'

If they were surprised to see Len and Trottie, they were even more surprised to see the two vociferous vegans tucking into rare fillet steaks.

'Shall I wave to them?' asked Georgia, mischievously. 'Just to let them know we've seen them.'

Charlie grinned. 'No, don't do that. I think it might be more amusing if we keep this to ourselves for the time being.'

Georgia picked up an asparagus spear and dipped it in her poached egg. 'The food here really is excellent. I'm not used to such decadence. It's usually pizza or pasta from the local takeaway.'

'What *are* you doing here, Georgia?' asked Charlie. 'At the commune, I mean. You don't strike me as a gullible lady, the sort to believe what someone says without questioning it.'

'Is that what you think this cult is about — naïve idealism? A blind belief that everyone is good?'

Charlie shrugged. 'What's your take on it, then?'

She thought for a bit. 'I think as long as there are people seeking answers to life's biggest questions, there will be receptive audiences for leaders who seem to provide the answers.'

'What, leaders like Solomon and Urbain — Major Mistake and Captain Cock-up?' Charlie laughed.

Georgia laughed too, then became serious. 'I've been there a month now, and I believe there's more to the Foundation than you might think, from first impressions. There are certainly some deeply troubled souls, battling with their personal demons. The problem is, I'm not sure this cult is the healthiest place to do it. Anyway, why are *you* here, Charlie? You don't seem a typical seeker of spiritual truth with a need to believe that life has a higher purpose.'

'Oh, I'm just here for the totty. A mate of mine told me there was plenty of it going spare. I'm what's known as a "player". Mind you, my idea of a night on the tiles isn't four hours of Scrabble with Howie and his missus.'

Georgia liked Charlie. She wasn't sure she should, but it was difficult not to. All the same, she didn't believe a word he said. Like her, he clearly had an ulterior motive for spending time with a bunch of misfits, and she vowed to find out what it was.

CHAPTER SEVEN

Now they had the identity of the dead man, the Murder Investigation Team started to look into his personal life, to see if they could find any clues that might have led to his death. Clive, head of the tech team, had obtained details of Carrington's finances from the accounts he'd had with various banks. Dawes firmly believed that Clive could hack into the Bank of England, if that's what was required.

'Sir Bixby was skint, sir. Not just broke but in shed-loads of debt. Several accounts overdrawn beyond the limit, all his credit cards maxed out, and according to his emails, his widow wasn't the only person he tried to borrow money from.'

'What did he spend all this loot on?' asked Malone.

'Dunno, Sarge. He kept drawing out large sums in cash. I can't find out what he did with it, though.'

'Another woman?' suggested Gemma Fox. 'It usually is.'

'Dear me, DC Fox, you have a very low opinion of men,' remarked Dawes. 'We aren't all lying, cheating, nasty bast . . . er . . . blokes of uncertain parentage.'

'If it was another woman, she was a bloody expensive one.' DC Williams was looking at the files.

'In my experience,' said Malone, 'when a bloke gets into that much debt, it's one, or sometimes all, of three things — drink, drugs and gambling.'

'Well, we already know from Big Ron—' Williams corrected himself — 'Sorry, Sarge, I mean, Doctor Hardacre — that the deceased's body contained a great deal of booze and LSD. So that's two of 'em taken care of.'

'Well, alcohol isn't that expensive, although I doubt if Sir Bixby drank cheap vodka,' observed Gemma, 'but the UK is being flooded with acid right now, for some reason.'

'No sign of him buying it online,' said Clive, checking his search history.

'No, but a man with his contacts could probably get someone else to buy it on the street for him,' said Gemma. 'It's one of the easiest drugs to smuggle — in liquid form or on squares of paper called tabs.'

'You seem to know a lot about it, young Gemma,' remarked Malone.

'Yes, Sarge. I studied it as part of my law degree. Not personally, you understand. I was working so hard and staying up so late, my life was one long trip anyway, without making it worse with drugs.'

'Are we any closer to finding Doctor Hardacre's trout lake?' asked Dawes. 'If we could find where he drowned, we might perhaps be able to draw some conclusions about how he ended up where he did.' He called across to DS Parsloe, who was the expert on the local territory.

'Norman, where's the nearest body of water to Richington Forest?'

Parsloe scratched his head. 'There isn't one, Jack. There's the Thames, of course, running through Teddington, Richmond and Kingston, but that's miles away. I'm guessing you're looking for something closer.'

DC 'Mitch' Mitchell was peering at a map on his screen. 'There's a bit of blue on here, sir. Very small, though.'

Parsloe looked at it, over his shoulder. 'That isn't a body of water — not as such. That's the lake on the old convent estate. Mind you, there aren't any nuns there these days. It was abandoned for a long time, then I believe the church passed it to some sort of New Age hippy cult, calling themselves the Foundation of the Free Spirit — all drugs and rock concerts, I shouldn't wonder. I'm surprised the old nuns haven't come back to haunt them.'

'Could you drown in it — this lake?' asked Malone.

'You could drown in a puddle, if someone stood on your neck,' said Parsloe.

'Might be worth taking a look, guv,' suggested Malone.

'I agree. In the meantime, Clive, could you do a background check of this Foundation of the Free Spirit? See if there are any skeletons in their cupboard.'

But before they could visit the home of the cult, either physically or virtually, another body turned up.

* * *

Councillor Mrs Amelia Hughes-Jones had been hot favourite for the next mayor of Kings Richington. Supported by her wealthy company director husband, Paul, she was a very public figure, always smartly dressed, immaculately made-up and with a lot to say. She was most active in developing council policy, to ensure it aligned with her lofty vision for the local area. Her resolute stance on budget setting was renowned among her fellow councillors, and she devoted a good deal of her time to scrutinizing their financial decisions. It therefore came as a massive shock to everyone who knew her, personally and politically, when she was found, naked and eviscerated, on the same chest tomb in Richington Forest where Sir Bixby Carrington had been discovered only weeks before.

Once again, police cordoned off the area, having only recently removed the tape from last time. Uniform and Scene of Crime Officers were searching for anything that might provide a clue to whatever new, unholy profanity had occurred.

'Bloody hell, Jack, what a mess.' A chastened Bugsy was visibly shaken at the appalling sight that had met them when they'd answered the urgent call. DC Williams, white faced, appeared from among the trees, where he had clearly been throwing up.

'Sorry, Sarge. It was bad enough finding Sir Bixby but — a woman? It's like Jack the Ripper.'

'It's all right, son. I was going to say, "You'll get used to it, in time," but you won't. None of us does. A sight like this is always stomach-churning, no matter how many times you witness it.'

'Who found the body, Aled?' asked Dawes, gently.

'A jogger, sir. Out for his morning exercise. He was running late, so he decided to take a shortcut through the forest. We've taken his statement and let him go. Nothing to suggest he had anything to do with what happened — just in the wrong place at the wrong time. Says he's never going to jog through the forest again.'

Dr Hardacre arrived soon after, accompanied by a clenched-faced Marigold Catwater. The doctor looked hard at the corpse. 'You know who this is, Inspector?'

'Yes, Doctor. I've seen her photograph in the *Echo* several times. It's Councillor Mrs Hughes-Jones.'

'Indeed it is. Amelia was a prominent figure in local government and a staunch supporter of many charities. You need to catch whoever did this, Jack.'

'We shall.' Dawes was emphatic. 'What can you tell me that will help, Doctor?'

'Like the last fellow in this situation, she didn't die here. She was brought here, already dead, before she was opened up. There are the same claw and bite marks and strands of the curly black hair, but again, this wasn't the work of a wild animal.' She gently lifted the head and examined the back. 'The post-mortem will provide more information, but I believe this is what killed her.' She indicated a bloody wound on the back of her head. 'Her skull is fractured.'

'Our old friend, blunt force trauma?' guessed Malone.

'That's right, Sergeant. But if I'm correct, it was caused by her head hitting a hard object and not the other way around. You'll have the pathology report as soon as possible.'

She gathered up her bag and strode off, followed by Miss Catwater carrying strands of curly black hair in an evidence bag.

* * *

George Garwood went to see Paul Hughes-Jones personally. Paul was a member of his Masonic lodge and Amelia had been a prominent member of Kings Richington society, so he felt it merited the personal attention of a Detective Chief Superintendent. The dead woman was also a good friend of Cynthia Garwood. They were all shocked at her demise — not least the manner of it.

'Paul, do you have any idea how Amelia ended up in Richington Forest?'

'None at all. She went out quite late that night, saying she needed to visit a local resident on council business. She didn't say what it was about and I didn't ask. She was very conscientious about her responsibilities as a councillor.' His voice broke and he had to pause for some moments.

'Did Amelia have any enemies?' Garwood asked, gently.

'Not enemies, George. Obviously, she faced some challenges from other members of Richington Council — she was a forthright woman who didn't suffer fools — but none of them would want her dead.' He faltered and took a large mouthful of the brandy that Garwood had poured for him. 'I think she might have had something on her mind lately. She'd been distant — a bit secretive. All the same, it's unthinkable that she should end up the way she did, naked and ripped open.' He set the glass down. 'George, you don't believe the story that's in the *Echo* — that she was killed by a wild beast, like Sir Bixby Carrington?'

'No, of course not. It's sheer nonsense. Sensationalism of the worst kind. I intend to have a serious conversation with the editor. Such misinformation scares the public and hampers police enquiries.' He stood up and put a reassuring hand on Paul's shoulder. 'I'm so sorry, old man. It's a terrible thing. I have my best officer on the case and a full team of detectives. We'll find whoever did this.' Privately, he was wondering whether Amelia might have been having an affair that went badly wrong. Only time would tell.

* * *

When he got home, Cynthia was watching the report of Amelia's death on the local news. The content was brief — just the announcement that she had died at the age of forty-one together with a potted account of her career. At the end, the correspondent asked that if anyone had any information concerning her death, they should come forward and speak to the police. Numbers were given.

She looked up as Garwood came in. 'George, what's going on? First Bixby and now Amelia, and in exactly the same way.'

The way George Garwood saw it was that desperate times called for desperate measures — so he poured himself a desperate measure of single malt from the bottle Jenny had given him in Scotland. It was going down fairly rapidly. 'How do you know it was exactly the same way?'

'Corrie Dawes told me. And it was in the early edition of the *Echo*. They want people who might know something to come forward.'

He sighed and sank into his armchair. 'That means the front desk will be inundated with halfwits, claiming to have seen black panthers and giant hounds.'

'Did Bixby and Amelia have anything in common?' Cynthia wondered.

'Not that I'm aware of. I doubt if they even knew each other.'

'Well, Corrie and I think there must be a connection somewhere. After all, it's too much of a coincidence that they should both be found dead in the same place and in the same condition.'

'Thank you, Cynthia. I'll make sure that the Murder Investigation Team benefits from your and Mrs Dawes's expert opinions.'

* * *

The mortuary was cold and dank, despite the soaring summer temperatures outside. Amelia Hughes-Jones's and Sir Bixby Carrington's post-mortems were similar in several respects with one or two striking exceptions. Dawes, Malone, Williams and Fox were present, suitably gowned. Dr Hardacre fixed them with her unequivocal stare.

'Councillor Amelia Hughes-Jones died of a fractured skull, as I predicted, between twelve and twenty-four hours ago. I can't be more precise due to the length of time the body has been out in the open. Death was caused by falling backwards onto the corner of something sharp, such as a kerb or step. I found traces of a fossiliferous, light yellowish-brown limestone in the wound — mostly likely local in origin. You often find it in old churches — chancel steps for example. Unlike Sir Bixby, the toxicology report shows no drugs or alcohol in her system. As you saw at the scene, another attempt had been made to make you think she had been the victim of an attack by a large animal. The curly black goat hair was the same. The bites and claw marks were made by the same implements. When you find them, I shall be able to draw a forensic comparison.'

'Nothing new then, Doc,' said Malone.

'Hold your horses, Sergeant. I haven't come to the interesting part.' She held out a hand and the inestimable Marigold put a DNA report in it. 'As is customary, SOCO took samples of DNA from the deceased and several more swabs from the slab on top of the tomb. As well as the fresh DNA from the unfortunate woman's body — pay attention, this is the important part — we found several, older DNA deposits from the same woman.'

The four police officers looked at one another, baffled.

Then Dawes said, 'Sorry, Doctor, but can you explain exactly what that means?'

'It means that Councillor Mrs Hughes-Jones left some of her DNA, in the form of dried vaginal secretions, on the tomb some time ago, before her demise.'

'Are you sure, Doc?' asked Malone, somewhat unwisely.

She raised her menacing eyebrows at the presumption of such an enquiry. 'Sergeant, if I were not sure, I shouldn't have said so.'

'Does DNA last that long, Doctor Hardacre?' asked Gemma Fox. 'I thought it would have degraded.'

'By no means. Researchers have estimated that under ideal conditions, DNA can last about six million years. Obviously, after about one and a half million years, it wouldn't be readable. In this case it was readable, and we have two samples of this woman's DNA, deposited on the tomb at least three weeks apart.'

'But that's impossible!' Dawes exclaimed. 'Why would there be traces of her DNA prior to her being placed there?'

'I keep telling you, Inspector. Finding the "how" and the "when" is my job — the "why" is down to you.'

* * *

Back in the incident room, Aled was updating the white-board with the new information and the whole of MIT was paying keen attention.

'Right, let's look at what we know,' said Dawes, with a confidence he didn't feel. 'We have two dead bodies, both prominent figures in the community. Causes of death were drowning and a fractured skull — either could have been an accident.' There were rumbles of dissent. 'Yes, I know what you're thinking. If they were accidents, how come they both ended up on a tomb in the heart of Richington Forest with their insides torn out instead of in the A&E department of Richington Infirmary? The pathologist's report gives us some clues as to their circumstances at the time they died. Our job is to find out if they were murdered, why the bodies were moved and who went to great pains to try to make us believe it was an attack by a wild animal. Right, team, get digging.'

They dispersed, noisily, each with different tasks to work on.

Bugsy was perplexed. 'This is a bloody weird one, Jack. I know we come up against some seriously twisted buggers in this job, but there doesn't seem to be any sense to this.'

'There will be, Bugsy. Maybe not sense as we see it, but it'll have made sense to someone's sick mind.'

CHAPTER EIGHT

Lilith was counting her winnings from the weekly poker school held, late at night, in one of the cloister buildings. It was a closed game — open only to invited participants. She was a good player but the odds were always on her side, thanks to the sophisticated method of cheating she had in place. Sometimes, for the sake of appearances, she lost, usually when the stakes were low, but when there was a considerable amount in the pot, she made sure she won it.

When she, Solomon and Urbain had set up the Foundation of the Free Spirit in Kings Richington, she wondered if the choice of location had been a mistake. On first acquaintance, the inhabitants of the peaceful and affluent town didn't immediately appear to be the kind of folk she sought. She had been pleasantly surprised — until now.

The reason they had closed down their previous enterprise — Followers of the Enlightened Mind — and moved swiftly on to new pastures was because many of the followers' minds had become rather too enlightened. This had resulted in diminished revenue and the very real risk of, at best, unpleasant accusations, and at worst, criminal charges. Then there had been the unfortunate 'accident'.

She locked the cash away in the safe, alongside a valuable Rolex watch, which a poker player had put in the pot on a previous occasion, when he had run out of cash. She knew such watches were numbered and traceable, and this one was engraved, so she hadn't dared try to shift it yet. Certainly, the owner was never going to redeem it.

When Sir Bixby Carrington had turned up at Solomon's Black Mass, Lilith had recognized him immediately, even in the black hooded robes. She'd remembered seeing his photograph in the papers some years ago, when he had received his knighthood for services to the government. He had been standing outside his expensive country seat, flanked by his elegant wife and two perfect children. Lilith's nose for money could sniff out a potential cash cow in minutes. What she hadn't expected was that it would end in so much tiresome trouble.

She had realized that he, more than most, would not want scandal. He had already gained a reputation in the community for drinking and gambling, which a man in his position could probably just about sustain without too much shame. Many of his peers had gone the same way in later life. Lilith had done a good deal of research, as she always did when selecting a new victim, and had discovered that his wife had left him and he lived alone. She had suspected, accurately, that the occasional night of anonymous and unbridled debauchery would appeal — as would an all-night poker school.

All that had remained was to ensure that the hidden cameras dotted around Richington Forest would capture his antics — particularly during the final orgy. To be absolutely sure, she had concealed herself in the trees with her own long-lens camcorder to catch the best shots. She smiled, remembering Carrington's face when she had shown him the footage. He had been cavorting with a middle-aged games' mistress from the local girls' boarding school. Both had been stark naked and assuming positions that even Vātsyāyana hadn't recorded. She wondered what Rushil would have made of it.

To begin with, Bixby had given in to Lilith's blackmail and paid up, albeit grudgingly, considering it fair remuneration on balance for services rendered. A brothel would have been cheaper but not as exciting or exclusive. But when she starting increasing the amount to an unsustainable sum, he had confronted her one night after the Black Mass. As Dr Hardacre had correctly assessed at the post-mortem, he'd had vast quantities of alcohol and LSD in his system during the orgy that night, enough to space out an elephant. In that state, he'd been clumsy and a befuddled brain rendered him unable to think clearly. Unwisely, he had boasted of a high-ranking friend in the police service and threatened to expose her and her illegal practices. It was then that she realized he was a loose cannon and could not be allowed to leave.

Having convinced him that he needed some fresh air, it had been a simple matter of walking him down to the lake and shoving him in. The disposal of the corpse, to avoid it becoming bloated and floating inconveniently to the surface, had been Urbain's idea. He'd picked up vague rumours about a beast on the loose in Richington Forest and exploited what he called 'the simple minds of the local peasants'.

It had been unfortunate that shortly afterwards, the Hughes-Jones woman had made a similar nuisance of herself. She had been in no doubt that being asked for a generous contribution to the Foundation was a veiled threat and she had more to lose than Carrington.

Lilith had arranged to meet her in the chapel after dark to discuss terms. She had obviously come straight from a council meeting, as she was wearing a business suit and white blouse. Lilith had shown her the video evidence of her role as the altar in Solomon's black sacrament followed by her brief but undeniable sexual intercourse with him. An angry exchange had resulted in an unseemly scuffle to grab the evidence. Lilith had pushed her away and Amelia, in her ridiculous high heels, had tripped and fallen hard on the chancel steps. Lilith had known at once that she was dead, and again, Urbain had disposed of the body in such a way that fed the lurid imaginations of the *Echo*'s readers. Amelia's clothes had gone the same way as Sir Bixby's — in the lake. Lilith had scrubbed the blood-stained steps and considered any potential danger had been averted. She was congratulating herself on the clever handling of what could have been two tricky situations, when Solomon burst in, closely followed by Urbain.

'Lilith, what are we going to do?' Solomon was agitated. 'They've found another body on the tomb. The *Echo* says she was ripped to pieces by animals. It's my fault! They were Astaroth's black hounds of hell. It was my invocation that brought them down upon her. I might as well have offered her up as a sacrifice.'

'Calm down, Solomon,' said Urbain. 'I keep telling you, it was no such thing.'

'What was it, then? Tell me that! You won't be so sure of yourself when the police come. They are unsympathetic to the black arts and deny the beliefs and desires of genuine Satanists, like myself.'

Urbain and Lilith exchanged glances.

'Now, why would the police come here?' asked Lilith. 'There's nothing at all to connect the Foundation to those two unfortunate deaths. The bodies were found in the forest, not inside our walls. If the police had any evidence that we were involved, they would have come here to question us, and they haven't, have they? Why don't you go along to the refectory and get Harriet to give you a nice cup of tea and a chocolate biscuit?'

Solomon glared at them both then strode away, muttering to himself. When he was out of earshot, Urbain faced Lilith. 'I know he's your brother and all that, but honestly, I think Sol's losing it. He's starting to believe in all that devil worship nonsense. He really thinks he can summon up demons from hell.'

'It's because he believes it that he's so convincing. You have to admit, he is good. We had ten more disciples at that last Black Mass. One of them was a High Court judge. It's just as well, since we've lost two of our most lucrative contributors in rapid succession.'

Urbain grinned. 'What's not to like? Sex, drugs and rock 'n' roll, with a bit of woo-woo thrown in! All the same, I think we should lie low for a while, until the noise dies down.'

'I agree. So far, there's nothing to implicate us in anything illegal, and the disciples aren't going to say anything, for obvious reasons. Don't worry about Solomon. I can handle him.'

'Fair enough. I guess we need him. After all, we can't really advertise for a replacement down the Jobcentre. *Wanted: an unfrocked priest, familiar with demonic possession. Must be able to conduct a Black Mass and referee a naked orgy.*'

Lilith laughed despite herself. 'It was the demonic possession that got him unfrocked in the first place. Turned out the bishop wasn't too impressed with Solomon's supplication to the incarnate spirit of Astaroth during Eucharist — to say nothing of the congregation. Several blue-rinsed ladies chased him from the church shouting, "*Heathen! Defiler!*" and beating him about the head with their handbags. He said it was the most terrifying ordeal of his life — far worse than summoning demons.'

* * *

As it transpired, keeping a low profile in order not to attract media attention ceased to be a problem, as something equally shocking hit the headlines of the *Echo* and the local television news. The dead bodies of a man and a woman had been discovered in their own home. The names were being withheld until the next of kin could be informed.

Uniform had received the 999 call from an hysterical postlady who had been trying to deliver a parcel to one of the large country houses in Richington Magna. It belonged to an elderly couple who were more or less housebound, with only a granddaughter to look after them. The postlady tended to look out for them, as she did several customers on her round. Not wanting to take the parcel back to the depot and unable to get a response from continual knocking, she had bent down and peered through the letter box, calling their names. There were blowflies buzzing around inside and the unmistakeable smell of decomposition.

The first thing she saw was the blood — a lot of it — splashed up the wall and spread across the hall floor. Then she had seen the old gentleman, lying on the hall carpet, with a kitchen knife sticking out of his chest. The blood was dark and congealed and he was clearly dead. She had wasted no more time but pulled out her phone and called the emergency services. Two uniformed police officers had arrived no more than ten minutes later to find the postlady sitting cross-legged on the grass, unable to do anything but point at the house.

Reluctant to smash the elegant front door, unless it became absolutely necessary, one of the officers had found an open window around the back and climbed through into the kitchen. He had jumped down from the sink, one foot landing in the cat's water and the other skidding on a pool of congealed blood. He had narrowly avoided treading on the arm of an elderly lady, also with knife wounds in her chest and stomach. Having established that the gentleman and his wife were beyond any help, the officers had cordoned off the crime scene and radioed the station for backup.

The Murder Investigation Team was deeply engrossed in the two Richington Forest deaths — two more corpses were just what they didn't need.

'Bloody hell, guv, is it open season on attacks by nutters?' Bugsy had hardly had time for more than two pork pies and a pasty for lunch. He was convinced he was borderline pastry-dependent, so took the precaution of grabbing a couple of sausage rolls from his office drawer and stuffing them in his pocket before they set off for the crime scene.

Dr Hardacre and SOCOs were already there, going through the now-familiar routine. 'No mystery about the cause and place of death, this time, Inspector. They were fatally stabbed, here in their own home, with a large blade.' She indicated a knife block on the work top. 'There's one missing — a large vegetable knife. I'm assuming that's the one our killer used. I'll test it back at the lab when I get it out of the poor chap's chest.'

'When did they die, Doc?' asked Bugsy.

'Difficult one, that. I'd say at least two weeks ago — could be more. I'm pretty certain the woman died first. I'll have a better idea when I've opened them up.' She nodded grimly. 'At least this time, someone hasn't done it for me.' She called across to a member of the SOCO team. 'Could someone catch a few of these *Calliphoridae* for me, please? It might help with the time of death.' She strode away.

The young lady tasked with catching the blowflies chastised Bugsy. 'Sarge, you're dropping flaky pastry all over the crime scene. Doctor Hardacre won't be happy if she finds some in her specimen pot.'

Bugsy grinned. 'Sorry, love.' He whispered to Jack. 'I don't think I've ever seen Big Ron when she *was* happy. I reckon it would be dead scary.'

Outside, DC Fox had found a chair for the traumatized postlady and given her a glass of water. She came across to Inspector Dawes. 'Sir, I think you should hear what the witness has to say. She found the bodies and called the police.'

Jack approached the whey-faced woman. 'Can you tell us exactly what happened here, please?'

'I've been delivering post around here for twenty years and I've never seen anything like this. It's such a respectable area.' Madge had stopped shaking but her voice was still wobbly. 'Who could do a thing like this? They were a lovely old couple — religious and law-abiding. To think I've been putting letters through the letter box, not knowing anything was wrong. It was only when this parcel came for them that I had to knock.' She sipped more water. 'Did they take much?'

'Did who take much?' asked Bugsy.

'The robbers. That's what it was, wasn't it? A robbery that turned nasty. Mr and Mrs Johnson must have disturbed them and been stabbed. Terrible society we live in. Time was, you could leave your doors open and nobody would rob you. I blame the government. There's no proper deterrent.

Murder someone and you get a room to yourself, all expenses paid, three meals a day and an Open University degree at the end of it.'

'Did they live alone, madam?' Jack stemmed the flow of righteous invective in the hopes of hearing something useful.

'No, I believe they have a granddaughter.' A terrible thought occurred to her. 'Oh dear, she isn't dead as well, is she?'

'No, madam, we haven't found any other bodies. Do you know the granddaughter's name?'

Madge frowned, trying to remember. 'No, I'm afraid not — only the initial, on her letters, you see. It was S. Johnson, if that's any help.'

'What about where she worked?' asked Bugsy.

'Oh, I don't think she had a job. She was only young — a teenager. Probably still at school, or college. I know the Johnsons were very proud of her. Her parents died when she was small and they took her on, even though they were middle-aged. They must have mentioned her name, but I'm blowed if I can remember it. You talk to so many people in my job. You don't remember them all. I've a feeling in the back of my mind that it was something unusual. No, it's no use, Inspector, it's gone.'

Jack decided it was time to give up. 'Could you give DC Fox here a description?'

'I'll try, but I didn't see her very often and young girls all tend to look the same these days.'

They left SOCO to their work and walked back to the car. 'No sign of a forced entry, guv,' observed Bugsy, 'although I guess whoever it was could have got in through the window, same as the uniform lads. No obvious signs of anything stolen, either. There were some nice pieces of silver and porcelain in the dining room and the old lady had some valuable jewellery. It was still on her dressing table. SOCO found a safe behind one of the pictures. There hadn't been any attempts to open it.'

'I wonder where the granddaughter is. She'll be next of kin and she'll have to be notified. It doesn't look like she's been home for a while or she'd have found the couple and raised the alarm.'

DC Fox caught them up. 'I looked in her room, sir. Everything's still there — her clothes, make-up, teddy bear on the bed, all the things a young girl might take with her if she was going away. Nothing to identify her, though. No mobile, no passport, and no laptop. You don't think that whoever broke in and killed the old couple have kidnapped her, do you, sir?'

'I'm not sure what I think at the moment, Gemma. We have to do what we're always telling the media we're doing — following all lines of enquiry. Let's hope SOCO comes up with something.'

'She could have gone backpacking around Thailand or somewhere, for all we know,' offered Bugsy. 'It's what young people do nowadays.'

'Wherever she is, the poor kid's going to get a terrible shock when she gets back,' predicted Dawes.

CHAPTER NINE

After a long process of unsuccessful checks and enquiries of schools, hospitals, the electoral register and any other source that might produce a result, Clive and his team of techies finally tracked down the granddaughter's identity — Summer Johnson.

'She left Richington Academy this summer, sir, aged seventeen. According to her head teacher, she was an anxious child, prone to bouts of nervous melancholy. Her parents were killed in a house fire when she was ten and she went to live with her grandparents. The teacher had no idea what Summer intended to do after leaving school as she had no qualifications and hadn't shown any aptitude for anything. She seems to have dropped off the radar, sir. No trace of her on any of the social media sites which you'd expect a seventeen-year-old to follow. She could be anywhere by now. Do you want me to put out a MISPER report?'

Dawes thought about it. Technically, Summer Johnson was classified as a high-risk missing person, being the possible victim of a crime or foul play. There was also the potential for her to be in need of medical attention and they had no pattern of her running away previously. She was also a child, within the law. Jack had a gut feeling about this one. He feared it might not end well. 'Do we have a photo of her, Clive?'

'Yep. I got one of her school photos from her head teacher. She's in uniform and it isn't very clear. I could enlarge it, sharpen it up a bit.'

'Yes, do that, please. Let the editor of the *Echo* have a copy. He isn't usually on the side of law and order but he might make an exception in the case of a missing girl. Make sure he doesn't print any connection to her grandparents and how they died. Tell him he'll be the first to get the full backstory, when it can be released.'

* * *

Charlie Updike was the first person in the commune to see the picture of Summer Johnson on the front page of the *Echo*, having access to an early edition. Although it was a poor likeness, he recognized her immediately. He went to find her but she wasn't in her room.

'Georgia, have you seen Summer?'

Georgia was typing something on her laptop and she closed it swiftly when Charlie came in. 'No, not since breakfast. She was as white as a ghost and just drank coffee. I think Lilith has taken her to the Lodge.'

'You mean the Old Barn where the Outlaws hold their secret meetings and we're not allowed in,' he joked.

Georgia laughed. 'That's right, and they scoff cream buns with lashings of ginger beer. I wonder if Solomon has a catapult.'

Charlie turned to go. 'If you see Summer, tell her I'd like a chat with her.'

Suddenly serious, Georgia stared at him. 'Why are you *really* here, Charlie?'

He stared back. 'I could ask you the same thing.'

Outside, Charlie kicked the Harley into life and sped down the track to the hut where he kept his mobile. He juiced it up with his charger and hit the button for the editor of the *Echo*.

'Hello, boss? That girl on the front page that everybody's looking for — Summer Johnson. She's here. Yes, I'm sure. She turned up a couple of weeks ago and they took her in. No, she's nothing to do with the other business. I was getting close to that, but it seems to have gone quiet since the cops found that last body. What do you want me to do about the girl? Yep, OK, I'm on it.'

* * *

Lilith had sensed trouble when Summer arrived, blood-stained and terrified, but even she hadn't foreseen quite how bad that trouble would turn out to be. She took the girl to the Lodge and made her a cup of tea, laced with one of Urbain's illegal substances, alleged to induce relaxation and honesty. That and the other 'merchandise' he peddled were part of what he claimed to be his 'pursuit of spiritual truth'. Lilith decided it was more the pursuit of a great deal of money, but there was no point in harbouring a drug dealer if you couldn't make use of his products.

'Summer, there's an article and a picture of you on the front page of the *Echo*. It seems the police are looking for you.' The last thing Lilith wanted was to attract the unwelcome attention of the police. However, the girl was clearly from a wealthy background and if there was enough money in it, Lilith was prepared to risk it.

'I expect they've found my grandparents,' she said, calmly.

'Why? Were they lost?'

'No,' she replied. 'They're dead. I killed them.'

Lilith caught her breath. Maybe this stuff of Urbain's induced fantasies rather than truths. She trod carefully. 'Why would you do that, dear?'

Summer looked straight into Lilith's eyes. It was a chilling experience. 'I had to. The voices insisted.'

'Whose voices were they?'

'The demons, of course. They're always with me — have been all my life. They tell me what to do.'

'I see. Did they give you a reason why you had to kill your grandparents?'

'Yes. It was because they were so religious, went to church a lot. At home, they said grace before meals and prayed at night before they went to sleep. They were always at it, telling me I had to lead a good Christian life, pray to Jesus and have faith in God.'

'And the demons didn't like that?'

'No, it made them angry. They were afraid it would influence me and I wouldn't listen to them anymore.'

'Summer, tell me how you did it.' Lilith was starting to feel decidedly uncomfortable. Even by her standards, this was evil on a whole new level.

'I was preparing vegetables for our evening meal. My gran came into the kitchen to see how I was getting on. The demons said, *Do it! Do it now!* So I stuck the knife in her and she fell on the floor. Then the demons said, *Quick! Do the other one!* I went into the hall where my grandfather was, and as he came towards me, I stuck the knife in his chest. Then the voices told me to run away, so I ran here.'

'Are the demons happy for you to be here?' asked Lilith. Having a conversation about voices in someone's head was bizarre, even by Lilith's warped standards.

'Yes, they say the conditions here are right.'

Lilith had to think fast. If this child was found guilty of murder, that would be the end of any inheritance and her share in it. 'What did you do with the knife, Summer?'

'Nothing. I left it sticking out of my grandfather's chest.'

No problem with fingerprints — she'd been chopping vegetables with it a few minutes earlier. 'I think we must assume that the police are going to trace you here and probably quite soon. There are some members of the cult who will see the appeal and feel they must report it.'

Summer frowned. 'What do we do?'

'I think it would look better if we were the ones to call the police first, rather than wait for them to track you down.'

'OK, but what shall I say?'

'I'll tell you what you're going to say. Listen carefully.'

* * *

DC Mitchell took the call. 'Sir, there's a woman called Lilith on the line — didn't give a surname. She wants to speak to whoever is in charge of the search for Summer Johnson.'

'OK, Mitch, put her through.' Dawes put his phone on speaker so the team could hear. 'This is Detective Inspector Jack Dawes. How can I help?'

'I understand you're looking for a missing girl, Summer Johnson?'

'That's correct. Can you give me your full name, madam?'

'Never mind that now, Inspector. Summer is here with us at the Foundation of the Free Spirit. We're looking after her.'

'I see. Could you bring her to the station? We need to speak with her urgently.'

'I think it would be best if you came here. She's fragile and would be more comfortable where she feels safe. I'm acting as her responsible adult.'

'Very well. We'll come straight there.' There was a click on the other end. Lilith had terminated the call.

Dawes called across to his head techie. 'Clive, you did a background check on this Foundation place. Did you find anything?'

'No, sir. Clean as a whistle. But they're a relatively new cult — only been going for a few months. From their website, I get the impression that it's a phoenix set-up.'

'What does that mean, son?' asked Malone.

'It's when a business has emerged from the collapse of another, usually through insolvency. It's perfectly legal to form a new company from the remains of a failed one, but there are rules. I've seen examples where unscrupulous operators running something dodgy have come close to police attention, so they shut up shop, move on and start up somewhere else under a new name.'

'Does this cult have proper accounts?' Bugsy's first instinct in any investigation was to follow the money.

'Yes, Sarge. Again, nothing suspicious. Each cult member makes a donation and running costs come out of that. There are tax returns, VAT, all the legal stuff. If they aren't genuine, they're very smart.'

'This Foundation is on the estate of the old convent,' DC Williams reminded them. 'Sergeant Parsloe reckons they have a lake. We were going to take a look in case that was where Sir Bixby drowned.'

'Two birds, young Taffy, two birds,' confirmed Malone.

CHAPTER TEN

Lilith showed them into the Foundation House rather than the Lodge — there was too much in there that she would rather the police didn't see. If they decided to get a warrant, of course, she'd have to shift some stuff a bit rapidly, but at the moment they had no obvious reason to want one and it would take them a while to find an amenable magistrate. She had dressed in her usual flamboyant style — wild, wavy hair, a long, flowing dress showing plenty of cleavage, and big hoop earrings. She wore a pendant on a chain around her neck — a silver talisman bearing the six-point Seal of Solomon.

Jack tried not to look at her splendid bosom. 'Lilith is an unusual name,' he began.

She smiled. 'Lilith was Adam's first wife, Inspector. She taught him the ropes. It's well-documented. "*Evil Lilith came to Adam against his will and became hot from him and bore him many demons.*" But she wouldn't accept an inferior role and demanded equality, especially sexually. When Adam wouldn't give it, she cursed him and left, to be replaced by submissive little Eve. Lilith is considered by some to represent female empowerment. Others claim she became a demon who seduces sleeping men.' She held Dawes's gaze and quoted: "'*She roams at night and goes all about the world and makes sport with men and causes them to emit seed.*'"

Having got rather more information than he bargained for, Dawes cleared his throat. 'Might we speak to Summer? I'm afraid we have some rather disturbing news for her.'

'If you mean the murder of her grandparents, she already knows. But I should let her explain. Go gently, please. She's still very traumatized. When she arrived, she was virtually catatonic. It was some time before we could persuade her to say anything and she still isn't eating properly.' She called through to the next room. 'Summer, would you come in now, please?'

Jack and Bugsy exchanged glances. They hadn't expected this turn of events. When Summer Johnson came in, they could see how thin and pale she was. She sat next to Lilith who held her hand.

'Summer, these officers need to ask you some questions. Don't be afraid. Just tell them the truth.'

Jack started the interview while Bugsy took notes. 'Summer, what can you tell us about the last time you saw your grandparents?'

She hesitated. 'I was upstairs in bed. I think I'd been asleep for a while but I was woken by a noise downstairs.'

'What sort of noise?'

'Shouting. A man's voice shouted "Tell us where the safe is!" Grandfather shouted back, "Never. Get out of my house!" Another man's voice, a different one, shouted, "We're not leaving without the money!" Then, I heard my grandmother scream, "You've killed him!"'

'Did you go downstairs? Could you describe the men?' asked Jack, with little expectation. The child must have been terrified.

'No, I was scared. I hid in my wardrobe in case they came upstairs. When I heard the front door slam, I supposed they must have gone. I only went down after it had been quiet for a long time. I don't know how long I was in there.'

'What did you see, love?' asked Bugsy, gently.

'My grandparents were dead, lying in pools of blood. My grandfather had our vegetable knife sticking out of his chest — the one I had used to chop carrots for supper.'

'Then what did you do?'

'I let myself out of the front door and ran.'

'That's when she turned up at our gates,' added Lilith. 'It was a filthy night, pouring with rain. She was soaked and crying. Obviously, I took her in and much later, when I realized the police were looking for her, I contacted you.'

'Why didn't you ask her who she was and what had happened to her until now?' asked Malone.

'Sergeant, we aren't called the Foundation of the Free Spirit for nothing. When people ask to join our commune, we don't interrogate them before we let them in. There are a number of reasons why people come here — many of them deeply personal and upsetting. They tell us what they want us to know and nothing more.'

'So you could have all manner of criminals and refugees from justice living here,' suggested Dawes.

She gave him a tepid smile. 'I hardly think so, Inspector. This is Kings Richington not the Costa del Crime. Now, if that's all, I think Summer should go and lie down. I think you'll agree, she's had a terrible experience for a young girl.'

'OK, madam, but we'll need to speak to her again, to obtain a written statement.'

After they'd left, Summer asked, 'How did I do?'

Lilith smiled. 'Well done. You even convinced me. Now, we just let the police run around in circles looking for non-existent murderers and when the coroner finally rules "murder by person or persons unknown", you'll be rich.' *And so will I*, she thought.

Outside, Jack and Bugsy met up with Aled and Gemma, who had taken the opportunity to wander around the extensive grounds before anyone could tell them not to.

'We found the lake, sir,' declared Gemma. 'And it does have trout in it. We met a couple who do the gardening for the commune — Howard and Harriet. The man had fished several out to cook for dinner tonight.'

'It's certainly deep enough to drown someone,' said Aled.

'What we really need,' said Dawes, 'is a sample of the water for Doctor Hardacre to analyse.'

Gemma grinned and produced a plastic bottle from her bag. It had originally contained still drinking water from an unlikely Highland Loch. It now contained cloudy lake water. She handed it over.

'Gemma, have I ever told you what an asset you are to the team?' asked Jack.

'Not recently, sir, but thanks anyway.'

As they drove away, Gideon, lurking in the bushes as usual, wondered about the significance of the water and whether he should mention it to Lilith. He decided against it. He didn't speak to anyone if he could avoid it. He'd come here to rid himself of demons, not to acquire more.

* * *

'Well, what did you make of Summer Johnson's statement, Bugsy? I thought it sounded genuine,' said Jack.

Bugsy pondered. 'I agree — only one thing didn't quite add up. She said she heard her grandmother scream, "You've killed him," meaning Mrs Johnson had seen the intruder stick the knife in her old man. Big Ron reckoned the woman died first and Mr Johnson died afterwards. The knife was still in his chest when we found him. The killer would have had to stab Mr Johnson, then pull out the knife, stab Mrs Johnson and put the knife back in Mr Johnson's chest. That doesn't make sense.'

'No, it doesn't, old friend. Maybe Summer just got confused. It wouldn't be surprising under the circumstances, but it's worth bearing in mind.'

* * *

'Have you had a good day, darling?' asked Corrie. Jack was late home as usual, but she had made slow-cooked pork, cider and sage hotpot, which chortled happily away in the oven until required. She decided she would even let him have some creamed potatoes with it, as a special treat.

The aroma of Corrie's excellent food reached him while he was still in the hall hanging up his jacket. He came in sniffing appreciatively.

'You look like one of the Bisto kids,' laughed Corrie.

'I'm too young to remember,' he said, dodging a swipe with her tea towel. 'As for it being a good day, we interviewed the granddaughter of the old couple who were murdered. Now that the next of kin has been notified, it'll be all over the *Echo*. We promised the editor he could have first crack at the story in return for helping to identify the girl.'

'Was she terribly upset?' asked Corrie, searching for apple sauce.

Jack thought about it. 'I'm not sure, really. I must have interviewed dozens of bereaved folks in my time — most of them as a result of murder — but she seemed unusual, somehow.'

'In what way? Surely people react in different ways to personal tragedy.'

'Yes, but that's just it. She didn't behave as though it was personal. It was as though she was on the outside looking in. Describing something that had happened to someone else.'

'Probably just shock. Once it dawns on her what has happened, she'll need support.'

Jack put a huge forkful of hot food in his mouth. He quelled it with chilled sauvignon blanc. 'She has plenty of that. She's living with that New Age commune in the old convent. The woman who runs it was clucking around her like a mother hen.'

Corrie put down her knife and fork. 'Cynthia Garwood reckons that place is well dodgy. She says there are all sorts of rumours among the ladies of the Inner Wheel Club about practices that go on there.'

'What sort of practices?' asked Jack.

'She wasn't specific, but I shouldn't be surprised if a few of the more daring ladies go there and . . . well, practise it — whatever it is.'

'I thought it was a bit unorthodox, even for a New Age cult. While we were there, a bloke in red leathers roared past us on a Harley Davidson, and there was a seriously suspicious character lurking in the shrubbery. Ideally, I'd like to get someone in there to have a poke around but we don't have any grounds for a warrant.'

Corrie thought about this but said nothing. She produced a strawberry mousse from the fridge and changed the subject. 'What about the Beast of Richington Forest killings? Are you any nearer to finding out who or what it is?'

'Well, it isn't a beast, that much we do know, not unless it's learned how to drown someone or bash them over the head then drag them into the heart of the forest. Professor MacDuff, the demonology expert, came over all canny when we told him about the pentacle on the tomb. I half-expected him to say, "Beware the powers of darkness" and "Save your soul, laddie."'

'What did Bugsy think?'

'You know Bugsy — if he can't see it, touch it or eat it, it doesn't exist.'

CHAPTER ELEVEN

Next morning, Corrie waited until Jack had left for work, then she called Cynthia Garwood, who answered straight away.

'Hello, Corrie? How are you? Is the Cuisine doing well?'

'Fine thanks, Cynthia. Business is booming — but the reason I'm phoning is to ask if you're still going to yoga classes?'

'No, unfortunately, and I really miss it. It's so good for you, Corrie. You sleep better, it lowers your stress levels, increases your strength and flexibility and improves your balance.'

'So why did you stop going?'

'The woman who ran it was showing us how to do the Warrior III pose, where you balance on one leg. She tottered over and put her back out. We got an ambulance to her but she's still in traction. I haven't been able to find anyone else.'

Corrie couldn't help smiling. Cynthia, bless her, was totally oblivious to the glaring contradiction between improved balance and tottering over. 'There's an advertisement in this week's *Echo* for a yoga class on the lawn of the old convent building. It's run by a chap called Rushil. I wondered if you'd come with me.'

'Of course, I will.' She hesitated. 'Is there an ulterior motive?'

Damn, thought Corrie. *Cynthia could always see right through me, even when we were at school.* 'Why would you think that?'

Cynthia laughed. 'Corrie, you always avoid any kind of exercise like the plague. The most energetic you ever get is when you're whipping cream. Why are we really going?'

'I just thought it wouldn't hurt to improve my fitness,' she lied. 'I still get twinges from my floating kneecap where you whacked it with a lacrosse stick.'

Cynthia giggled. 'Corrie, we were twelve. You must have got over it by now. Tell me why we're going.'

'Jack and the team are investigating one of the members of the Foundation of the Free Spirit. They're trying to find out who killed her grandparents.'

'Yes, I saw her on the front page of the *Echo*,' said Cynthia. 'Poor little sausage — it said she was seventeen but she looked just a child. It seems her parents died in a house fire when she was ten. Now, I guess she doesn't have anyone.'

'Jack said the woman who runs the Foundation is looking after her until they decide what to do with her. Apparently, her grandparents were pretty well off, so she'll inherit quite a lot of money when she hits eighteen.'

'All the same,' said Cynthia, 'money doesn't replace your friends and family, does it? I still haven't come to terms with the death of Amelia Hughes-Jones. She was a useful member of the council — actually got things done. And she was tremendous chums with the members of the Inner Wheel Club. We can't understand who would want to kill her and in such a horrible way. And poor Bixby. He was a good friend of ours, years ago, before he started to go downhill and we drifted apart.'

'I know,' agreed Corrie. 'It was ghastly the way they were left. Jack's on the case. If anyone can get to the bottom of it, he can.'

'Does Jack think the Foundation has something to do with it? I shouldn't be at all surprised. Several of my ladies have heard rumours about what goes on there.'

'Jack hasn't said as much, in so many words, but he said he'd like someone who isn't a police officer to have a snoop around inside the convent.'

'So that'll be us! Jolly good! Sleuthing again — you and me. Sign us up for the yoga class. Top-hole!'

'Not a word to George and Jack, though,' cautioned Corrie. 'You know what they're like if they think we're interfering.'

'Absolutely. Mum's the word.'

* * *

Rushil's yoga class started at eleven o'clock on Friday morning, when George and Jack would be at work. Cynthia was right: Corrie avoided physical exercise as much as possible and had nothing sporty to wear, so Cynthia had lent her some shiny, dark purple yoga pants and a matching shirt. She'd lost weight since she bought them and they were now far too baggy. But Corrie was at least two sizes bigger than Cynthia, so they were still a bit on the tight side. Moreover, they were different shapes. Cynthia was hourglass, Corrie — on the stocky side of welterweight — was more goldfish bowl.

She'd decided to put on the outfit before she went, to avoid any embarrassment. She struggled into it in the back room of Coriander's Cuisine.

'How do I look?' she asked Carlene.

'Er . . . very . . . er . . . unusual, Mrs D.'

'No, seriously. What do I look like?'

'Honestly?'

'Honestly.'

'Like a giant grape on legs.'

Corrie giggled. It was in a good cause and once they'd had a snoop, she wouldn't have to go again.

* * *

When they arrived, a good crowd of ladies had gathered and spread out across the lawn with their yoga mats. Corrie and

Cynthia chose places right at the back of the class, so they could slope off unnoticed and have a look around.

Rushil, barefoot and wearing a long white tunic, glided silently across the lawn towards them.

'I say,' whispered Cynthia. 'He's very handsome, isn't he?'

'We're here to work,' admonished Corrie. Then, on second glance, 'Yes, he is, rather.'

Rushil greeted everyone with his customary 'Namaste' then circled the class, ringing a bell to cleanse the area with sound. It was his practice to commence with *Savasana* — the corpse pose — resting like the dead, to quieten busy minds and transition into the moment. Soon, everyone was lying flat on their yoga mats, eyes closed and completely relaxed. At the front, Rushil was in *Sukhasana* pose, sitting cross-legged with his eyes shut. He had chanted the seed mantra three times — 'Omm, omm, omm' — then invited the students to connect with him in a spiritual exchange. He intoned the questions and the class chanted the responses.

'As we close our eyes to old endings, we must open our hearts to the power of new beginnings. Who is man?' he asked.

'The reflection of the Eternal Light,' they replied.

'What is the world?'

'A wave on the Everlasting Sea.'

Corrie didn't have a clue what they were talking about, but this was the perfect opportunity to sneak away without being noticed. She opened one eye and squinted across at Cynthia, who was snoring gently.

Corrie kicked her. 'Cynthia,' she hissed. 'Wake up, we're supposed to be snooping.'

Her eyes flew open. 'Oh yes. Sorry.'

They scrambled to their knees, grabbed their belongings and slunk away, concealing themselves in the surrounding greenery.

'Where shall we start?' asked Cynthia.

'We're looking for anything that might connect Bixby and Amelia with this place. If they're running something dodgy here, I doubt they'd do it openly in the Foundation House, in full view of the inmates.'

'I think they're called members,' said Cynthia. 'They're not convicts.'

'Some of them might be,' argued Corrie. 'Let's explore the outbuildings — there are loads of them. I reckon that's where any funny business would happen.'

Cynthia nodded. 'On an estate this big, you could get up to all sorts of illegal stuff without even the cult members knowing about it. Has Jack interviewed any of them?'

'No, only the young girl. He doesn't have a good enough reason to interrogate the others. Yet. That's why we're here. We'll start by casually walking down the lane and having a nose around the main buildings. Then we'll look at the far ones.'

The chapel was open, so they went inside.

'Doesn't look like it's used very often,' said Corrie. 'There's nothing on the altar, no candles or a cross.' She ran a finger along one of the pews. There was a good deal of dust. 'You'd expect people who have come here to find inner peace and some kind of answer to life's vicissitudes would spend a lot of their time in a chapel.'

'I can imagine the nuns in here, singing and kneeling in prayer,' observed Cynthia. She had a tendency to drift off into a fantasy world. 'Have you ever wondered what it would be like to be a nun?'

'Not recently.' *Mind you*, she thought, *I'd look rather better in a nun's habit than this yoga outfit.*

They were about to leave when Corrie noticed that the stone steps around the chancel had been cleaned fairly recently. *Why*, she wondered, *would you clean only one part of a chapel and not all of it?*

Outside, they had reached the Lodge with its 'No Entry' signs. Corrie tried to look in through the windows but all the blinds were down. She tried the door but it was locked. 'Damn. I'd have liked to look in there.'

'It's probably just the staffroom,' said Cynthia. 'Nothing sinister there. After all, you see lots of doors in shops with

"Staff Only" on them. It doesn't mean the assistants are in there murdering somebody. Come on, we've got lots more snooping to do.'

Some time later, they had explored the quadrangle and peered into all the cloister buildings. Satisfied that the closest outhouses contained nothing more suspicious than old farm implements, what looked like black sacks and old animal skins, they headed out into the parkland, intent on doing a thorough job by examining the huts on the outskirts. As they approached the gardening hut, a young man on a red motorbike came roaring down the track towards them. They leaped smartly out of the way as he shot past. He raised a hand and shouted something unintelligible.

'I wonder who he is,' Cynthia said.

'I believe he came out of that hut over there. Let's look inside.'

Having thought they might have found something useful, Corrie was disappointed to see only gardening tools, an old wheelbarrow and a claw tool she assumed was for raking up leaves. 'I wonder what he was doing in here? It can't have been anything dodgy or he'd have locked it up.'

'Maybe he's the gardener,' suggested Cynthia. 'Look, there's a lake with water lilies and flag irises. Isn't it pretty? In fact, the whole place is rather lovely — calm and peaceful. You can see why people might want to come and chill out here.'

Corrie nodded. 'I agree. Right now, it's hard to imagine anything criminal going on.'

'Maybe it is simply a genuine case of kind people running a retreat where people can stay for a while to heal their mental health,' said Cynthia.

Corrie frowned. 'If Jack says his copper's nose twitched when he was here, you can bet there's something going on. I've never known him to be wrong. Let's just look in that last building — the big one right back off the road. Then we'll go home.'

When they got to it, they couldn't see anything. It was boarded up and securely locked, but chinks of light shone through the cracks and they could hear some kind of machinery running inside.

'What do you suppose that is?' asked Cynthia. 'A generator of some kind, in case of a power cut?'

Corrie shook her head. 'It wouldn't be much use all the way out here. How would they connect it up to the Foundation House?' She paused, then put her nose to the crack in the door. 'Smell that.' She stood back to let Cynthia have a sniff.

'I can smell something musty,' she said, eventually. 'Reminds me of the time when George and I were touring Canada. We got out of the car to have a picnic in the countryside and left the doors open. A skunk ran right through it, spraying. It didn't half stink. We couldn't get rid of the smell, whatever we did. Had to sell the car in the end.'

Corrie sniffed again. 'I've smelled it before. It's not that sort of skunk, Cynthia. Someone is growing marijuana in there.' She stood back, the better to see the size of the building. 'And a hell of a lot, by the looks of it. We've finally found something illegal that will give Jack a reason to search. Come on, let's go, before someone catches us.'

As they turned to leave, Corrie spotted it. She flattened herself against the wall, paralysed with fear.

'What's the matter?' asked Cynthia. 'You've gone a funny colour.' She followed Corrie's gaze and gulped — too scared even to scream. A huge, dark shape, the size of a well-built pony, was galloping down the track towards them. As the beast came closer, it let out a deep, throaty roar.

'Don't move,' muttered Corrie through clenched teeth. 'It might ignore us and go straight past.' But of course, it didn't. Goliath was delighted to have found two new visitors and welcomed them in his usual manner. He leaped up, put his paws on Corrie's shoulders and looked down at her with a canine grin. She braced herself against the wall but could feel her legs giving way under his weight. Bravely, Cynthia tried to pull him off, but thinking she wanted to play, he left Corrie and wrestled Cynthia to the ground with consummate ease. In Cynthia's mind, the Beast of Richington Forest was about to devour her. Poor George would have to identify her chewed-up remains.

'Can I help you, ladies?' said a smooth voice behind them. Urbain had spotted the two women when they had walked past the Foundation House. When he hadn't seen them come back, he had gone to see what they were up to. He was being ultra-cautious about strangers since the business with the bodies in Richington Forest. It was probably nothing, though. Members of Rushil's yoga class often wandered off, usually looking for the loo. He wasn't surprised. All that bending and stretching must play havoc with your bladder. He grabbed Goliath's collar and pulled him off. 'Stop it, Gollie. The ladies don't want to play.'

'Hello,' said Corrie, struggling to her feet and trying to sound confident. She was acutely aware that she was still dressed like a grape, but now she was covered in doggy drool as well. It wasn't her best look. 'I'm sorry if we're trespassing. Just needed to stretch our legs — those yoga poses affect my floating kneecap terribly. We're just going to find the loo. Come on, Cynthia.' She hurried away.

'Nice doggy.' Cynthia gave his massive head a cautious pat. She scurried after Corrie. 'Blimey, that was close,' she said, when they were out of earshot. 'What an enormous animal. I wonder who the bloke is.'

'Well, he isn't the gardener,' said Corrie. 'Did you see his hands? All soft with beautifully manicured nails. Let's get out of here before he lets the dog loose.'

After they'd gone, Urbain looked at the building that they had found so interesting. Needing to keep a low profile, he rarely strayed this far from the convent and hadn't noticed it before. Like Corrie, he could smell something — something very familiar. Unmistakeable, in fact, in his line of business. He wondered if Lilith knew.

* * *

'Yes, of course I knew,' she said, when he tackled her. 'It belongs to Len and Trottie. It was part of our arrangement when they came here. They were looking for somewhere to set up a cannabis farm, no questions asked. This place is ideal. Don't look so shocked. A new government report estimates that 500,000 people grow cannabis in the UK — roughly one person on every street. I was hardly going to turn down a good business deal.'

'And I suppose you get a generous cut of the proceeds?' he said.

'Of course. Don't tell me you're going to come over all righteous — you're a functioning drug dealer, for goodness' sake.'

Urbain shrugged. 'Not at all. I just think I should get a share.'

Lilith frowned. 'Who were these women you disturbed outside the cannabis shed? Should we be concerned?'

'No, just a couple of menopausal females from Rushil's yoga palaver, desperate for the loo. Completely harmless.' He laughed. 'Goliath scared the shit out of them. I doubt they'll come back.'

All the same, thought Lilith, *time we turned the hash into cash.*

CHAPTER TWELVE

When Jack came home that night, Corrie was wondering how to tell him what she and Cynthia had found without being accused of interfering. It was true she'd been in a few scrapes in the past — some of them dangerous — but it had always been with the best of intentions. At least this time, she'd come away relatively unscathed and with some useful information.

Jack knew she'd been up to something as soon as he came through the door. Steak and kidney pudding? On a weekday? With roast potatoes?

'Cynthia and I went to a yoga class today,' Corrie began, innocently enough.

'Yoga? You?' exclaimed Jack. 'But you hate exercising. I remember the time Carlene tried to get you to go to salsa classes with her. You said you didn't mind making salsa but you drew the line at dancing it.'

'Yes, but yoga's different. It's about flexibility and connecting your body to your . . . er . . . what's-its-name, and . . . er . . . learning to live in the . . . er . . . thing.'

'Bugsy says it's mostly about learning to hold in your farts.'

'What does Bugsy know? I bet he's never been to a yoga class in his life.'

'He has — he went with Iris. Only once, though. She was trying to shift some of his belly fat before the police fitness test. Everything went OK until they were lying down and the instructor told them to relax every muscle in their bodies. Apparently, Bugsy's mat vibrated.'

Corrie giggled. 'Oh dear, poor Bugsy.' She gave Jack a sideways glance. 'Don't you want to know where the class was?'

Jack poured some wine and picked up his knife and fork. 'Go on then.'

'It was on the lawn at the old convent.' She served him a large portion of pudding. 'I went with Cynthia, and guess what we found when we were looking for the loo.'

'I've no idea.' He gave her a stern look. 'Corrie, you weren't snooping, were you?'

'Well, only a bit. You said you wanted someone who wasn't a copper to have a poke around.'

He groaned in despair. 'I know that's what I said but I didn't mean you and Cynthia. It always ends badly. Look what happened the last time you and she did some sleuthing — she shot Carlene in the leg and you emasculated a Romanian gangster.'

Corrie ignored that as a gross exaggeration of an unfortunate incident that could have happened to anyone. 'You needed a reason to go in there and search and we found one. Jack, they're growing cannabis. I don't mean a pot plant — no pun intended — I mean a whole farm. It's immense. Must be making them a fortune.'

'How do you know? Did you see it?'

'No, the building was boarded up, but I could smell it.'

'Corrie, I can't go marching in there without a warrant because my wife thinks she smelled cannabis. Did you find anything that connects the cult to the two murders?'

'Not really. We were knocked down and jumped on by a huge dog. Cynthia thought it might be the Beast of Richington Forest.'

'That would be the mastiff that found Sir Bixby's corpse,' said Jack. 'He's quite harmless and anyway, there is no "beast". Can you remember anything else?'

Corrie pursed her lips in thought. 'No. It all seemed rather pleasant and peaceful. A young man in red leathers came roaring towards us out of the potting shed, on a Harley Davidson. Cynthia reckoned he was the gardener. And there was a smarmy-looking bloke, about forty, in an expensive suede jacket and designer jeans who rescued us from the dog. We told him we were looking for the loo.' She paused, trying to remember anything else that might be useful. 'There was a lake with fish and water lilies and a well-kept vegetable garden. The chapel was a bit grubby and needed a good clean, apart from the chancel steps. Someone had washed them. Very thoroughly.'

'Did you happen to notice what type of stone the steps were made of?'

'Why? Is it important?'

'It might be.'

'I haven't a clue — I'm a chef, not a stonemason.'

'What colour was it?' he prompted.

She cast her mind back, trying to picture it. 'It was sort of light brown, kind of yellowy, like toasted cheese or the top of a warm sponge cake. I only noticed because it was the one bit of the chapel that was clean. Sad little place, really. No flowers, no candlesticks on the altar, no cross. It didn't look as though a service had been held there since the nuns left. I'm sorry, Jack, I haven't been much help, have I?'

'You've been more help than you realize, my darling.' Not for the first time, Jack thought what an excellent witness Corrie would make. He looked greedily at the steak and kidney pud. 'Any chance of a second helping?'

All through the meal, Jack's brain had been in overdrive. The convent lake had fish and water lilies, according to Corrie. Big Ron had found traces of trout scales and water lily petals on Sir Bixby's body. If the water sample that

Gemma had taken from the lake matched the water found in Sir Bixby's stomach, and if the stone chancel steps matched the fragments found in the wound in Amelia Hughes-Jones's head, they'd have a connection between the murders and the Foundation. They were big 'ifs' and there could be all kinds of explanations — but it was progress of a sort.

* * *

Next morning, Jack arrived at the station, keen to see what results the lab had found about the water from the lake.

'Have we had the report on that sample yet, Aled?'

'Sorry, sir,' replied DC Williams. 'I have enquired, but Doctor Hardacre said they were still testing it. Well, actually she said, "Hold your water, young man. This is a laboratory not an assembly line. We don't crank out lab reports like wing mirrors on a Volvo."'

Clive, however, had some very interesting news. 'Sir, I've been watching the CCTV footage from outside the Johnsons' house on the night they were murdered.'

The team gathered behind him to watch. 'This is Summer Johnson coming out of the front door after the murders. She has blood on her jeans and she's in a hurry.'

'I'm not surprised,' said Bugsy. 'She's just had a terrible shock and she doesn't know that the killers aren't still lurking around.'

'She couldn't be sure how long she'd been hiding in the wardrobe,' added Gemma.

Clive kept the footage running. 'She sprints off in the direction of the convent. She isn't carrying anything, no phone nor handbag. Look at the time. It's only half past six — not yet dark.'

'I see what you're getting at, son,' said Bugsy. 'In her statement, she said, "I was upstairs in bed. I think I'd been asleep for a while but I was woken by a noise downstairs." Bit early to be in bed asleep, wasn't it?'

Clive nodded. 'That's what I thought, Sarge. The statement and the CCTV don't tally.'

Jack was puzzled. 'Where's the rest of it, Clive?'

'That's all of it, sir. There isn't anything else on the video. No robbers breaking in to commit the murders or legging it afterwards. No record of anyone going in or out that night other than Summer Johnson running away at six thirty.'

It went quiet while the most obvious explanation sunk in. Nobody wanted to confront the dreadful scenario of a teenager slaughtering the grandparents who had taken her in and cared for her. There had to be another explanation.

'But why?' asked Gemma, articulating what they were all thinking. 'Why would she do a terrible thing like that?'

'I think it's time to bring her in — away from the influence of that blasted Foundation,' decided Jack. 'We'll get someone from social services to act as responsible adult. This young lady has some serious explaining to do, not least the discrepancy that you picked up, Sergeant, about which of them was stabbed first. Her statement said it was her grandfather — Doctor Hardacre said her grandmother died first.' Then Jack had a sudden thought and a not very comfortable one. 'Clive, could you dig out the coroner's report on her parents' deaths from around seven years ago, please?'

* * *

Lilith was not at all happy when Dawes and Malone arrived at the Foundation unannounced and intending to take Summer down to the station.

'She's told you everything she remembers. I really think you should leave her alone.' Lilith didn't like the way events were going.

'We just need to clear up a few inconsistencies in her statement,' said Jack. 'DC Fox is here to accompany her in the police car.'

'Are you arresting her?' asked Lilith.

'Not yet,' replied Jack, somewhat ambiguously. 'Could you fetch her, please?'

When Summer appeared, she had dark shadows under her eyes from lack of sleep. She was still pale and painfully thin. Soft-hearted Bugsy felt sorry for the child, despite what they suspected she may have done.

She turned to Lilith. 'Will you come with me?'

'I don't think that will be necessary,' said Jack, quickly. 'DC Fox will look after you until we get to the station, and you'll have a social worker and a solicitor to advise you.'

Although he occasionally cut a few corners, in this case, Jack knew instinctively that it was vital to do everything strictly according to the book. This interview was shaping up to be a critical one.

After they'd gone, Lilith took stock of the situation. She was glad they hadn't wanted her to go to the station with Summer. The prospect of making any money from her was becoming increasingly unlikely. The last thing she wanted was any further intrusion by the police into the business of the Foundation. It was time, she decided, to keep her head down and leave Summer to the police. Of course, there was always the possibility that the girl would eventually tell the truth. In which case, she might also tell them that Lilith had told her to lie. Easy enough to deny, particularly in view of her 'voices'. They might just as easily have told her to lie. Summer was clearly mentally unstable, and it would be a case of an unhinged girl's word against Lilith's.

* * *

Back at the station, Summer was taken to the family room to speak with the social worker and solicitor. In the meantime, Jack and Bugsy read the coroner's report on the deaths of Summer's parents that Clive had tracked down. On the night they died, they'd had a party to celebrate their wedding anniversary. Guests interviewed at the time stated that the couple had consumed a good deal of alcohol. This was confirmed by the pathologist at the post-mortem. In addition, both the Johnsons had been heavy smokers.

Fire investigators had concluded that discarded ciga-rettes were the most likely cause of the fire, having found several burned out on a pile of newspapers alongside a box of matches. These, in turn, had ignited the curtains and the whole house had gone up before the fire service could get the blaze under control. The couple had died in their bed from smoke inhalation. Returning his verdict, the coroner had declared it a 'regrettable accident'. He stated that it was a difficult case and the evidence was harrowing. He offered his condolences to their young daughter for the tragic loss of her parents. Neighbours had found ten-year-old Summer wandering in the garden in her nightclothes. They had taken her in until her grandparents had arrived to fetch her. Police said there was nothing to indicate the fire had been started deliberately.

'What do you reckon, Bugsy?' asked Jack.

Bugsy sniffed. 'Looks pretty straightforward on the face of it. But what do you make of this bit in the police report? It says they found a chair, burned out, underneath the smoke alarm. It had been pulled off the ceiling and the batteries had been taken out. Their assumption was that the Johnsons had intended to put in new ones, but for some reason, they had forgotten.'

'Is there any record of what the child said at the time?' asked Jack.

Bugsy scrolled through. 'Can't find one,' he replied. 'Probably considered too young. Are you thinking what I'm thinking?'

'Almost certainly. But I don't want to believe it.'

* * *

Fortunately for Lilith, by the time Summer was interviewed by Dawes and Malone, she had forgotten her spurious ver-sion of events. Both the social worker and her solicitor had accurately assessed her severe and unstable mental condition. They decided it was in her best interests to tell the truth. Whatever the outcome, she would be deemed unfit to plead and would, in all probability, end up in a secure hospital until someone decided she was cured — if she ever was.

Jack began cautiously. 'Tell us what happened on the night your grandparents died, Summer. We don't believe robbers broke in during the night.'

She seemed calm and rational — as though it was perfectly reasonable to have done what she did. 'There weren't any robbers. I killed them. I had to.'

'But why?' asked Jack. 'They loved you and took care of you.'

'My demons told me to do it. I have to do whatever they say.'

'Did they explain why you had to stab them?' Jack was stunned, faced with such evil in so young a girl.

'They didn't like all the praying and going to church. They said it was bad for me. Harmful.'

'What do these demons look like, dear?' simpered the social worker.

Summer regarded her with scorn. 'I can't see them, silly! I only hear them — in my head.'

'Did the demons tell you to kill your parents, too?' asked Jack, dreading the answer.

'Oh yes. I told my father and mother about the voices, but they didn't believe me. They said I was telling lies just to get attention. The demons were very angry. They said my parents should burn in hell. They told me how to unscrew the smoke alarm and take the batteries out. Then I set fire to the house with some matches and newspapers. It went rather well. The demons were pleased. They like a good fire.'

'Why didn't you tell anyone that you set fire to the house?' asked Bugsy, shocked.

She looked at him, puzzled. 'Nobody asked me.'

CHAPTER THIRTEEN

With the weekend looming, Coriander's Cuisine was busy with orders for posh suppers for an evening in and Chez Carlene was fully booked by young folk wanting an equally posh supper for an evening out. Corrie and Carlene were planning the food and the sous-chefs were busy preparing it. The kitchens in the unit were buzzing.

'Mrs D, how did you and Mrs Garwood get on at your yoga class at the old convent?' Carlene looked up from the menu that she and Antoine were putting on that night. The couple's mastery of culinary techniques and the high-quality produce they used were some of the qualities that had gained them a Michelin star. As far as the customers were concerned, it was the taste of the food and a first-class dining experience that ensured the bistro was invariably fully booked.

Corrie laughed. 'We didn't do much yoga — none at all, in fact. But we did have a good snoop around the estate and nearly got devoured by a dog in the process.'

'What sort of dog was it?'

'A bloody great big one with slavering jaws.' Corrie grinned. 'Well, maybe it was just drooling because it was pleased to see us. It didn't really attack.'

Carlene frowned. 'If it was drooling, it was probably wondering what you'd taste like. I reckon that convent must be a seriously random place. We get some of the cult people in the bistro and in Corrie's Kitchen. They aren't at all like I imagined they'd be.'

'Why aren't they?' asked Corrie. She put down the meat mallet that she was about to use to bash some chicken breasts into escalopes and stuff with haggis. They were for Professor MacDuff's favourite Caledonian Chicken. He had phoned and explained, rather coyly, that he was entertaining a lady friend that evening and he wanted to impress her. Corrie was to deliver the food ready for him to serve. He had to be sixty if he was a day, and Corrie thought it was romantic. 'How are the cult people different to what you expected?'

'I don't know anything about all that New Age malarkey but I always imagined that the people who signed up to it would be . . . well . . . fed up with their lives and looking for a higher purpose — like I was, when you gave me my first job in catering, Mrs D.'

Corrie thought this was interesting. Carlene was a shrewd young lady and her observations might just help Jack with his enquiries into the deaths. He was still convinced they were associated in some way with the Foundation of the Free Spirit.

'We had a couple in the bistro the other night,' said Carlene. 'They came in very late and asked whether we did vegan food, so I gave them our vegan menu. He said to her, in a dead phony accent, "Eh oop, loov, does tha fancy marinated kale?" Then they burst out laughing and ordered rare fillet steaks and chips — in normal voices. I mean, what's that all about?'

'How did you know they were members of the cult?' asked Corrie.

'Foundation people have their room keys on a fob around their necks. They're not all fruitcakes, though. There was a couple in around the same time who certainly didn't belong in a home for loony tunes.'

'Why do you think that?' asked Corrie, amused.

'I overheard some of their conversation. I wasn't eavesdropping, Mrs D, but you know how it is when you're serving food. People do one of two things — they either stop talking until you've gone or they carry on, like you're not there. These two went on discussing the commune. He asked her what she was really doing there, because she didn't seem the gullible type. She said, did he think that was what the cult was about — naïve idealism? She reckoned there were some deeply troubled souls battling with their demons and the commune wasn't the healthiest place to do it. Then she asked him why he was there and he said he'd only come for the totty, but I could tell she didn't believe him. I had to clear their starters then, so I didn't hear any more.'

Corrie digested this information. 'That's interesting, Carlene. It strikes me that some people there have a different agenda from what you'd expect.' She made a mental note to tell Jack. Added to what she and Cynthia had seen, it might be useful.

* * *

On Saturday morning, Chief Superintendent Garwood called an emergency meeting of the MIT and Uniform officers. It was a full turnout. Everyone was keen to find out what new challenge faced them. Speculation was rife, particularly among the younger officers.

'I reckon the old man's got the wind up. Four deaths on our patch won't look good on the monthly returns.'

'He'll be ordering industrial quantities of indigestion tablets.' There was a smatter of sniggering.

'Two of 'em — the posh murders — still not solved.'

'At least we got to the truth behind Mr and Mrs Johnson's deaths, gruesome though it was.'

Bugsy carried his mug of tea and a bacon roll over to where Jack was sitting. 'What's this all about, Jack? I was supposed to be taking Iris food shopping this morning.'

Jack imagined food shopping was a priority in the Malone household, whereas he was more than adequately fed by the head chef of Coriander's Cuisine. 'I've no idea. Garwood just told me to make sure everyone attended, as we had a special job on.'

The troops stood up as Garwood entered the room. He waved them back down. 'We have an important role to play tomorrow. Members of Richington Council, supported by various other local organizations have become agitated by scurrilous reports in the *Echo* of wild beasts and demons in Richington Forest. As a result, they have decided to arrange an exorcism.'

There were exclamations of derision and disbelief.

'Yes, I agree, the whole idea is ludicrous. Nevertheless, as police officers, we have been asked to provide a presence to ensure the procedure is carried out in a lawful way and without any breaches of the peace. I want officers spread out around the edge of the clearing where the two bodies were found. The exorcism is to be carried out by Father Bartholomew, a retired priest, at ten o'clock tomorrow morning. Your senior officers will give you individual orders. Thank you.' He strode out.

'Blimey, I didn't see that coming,' said Bugsy.

'Neither did I,' agreed Jack. 'What exactly do they imagine they're going to exorcize?'

'If you believe the reports we get on the desk,' said Sergeant Parsloe, 'werewolves with fangs, vampires in cloaks and a big black thing with horns, curly fur and a rotting smell. The old padre has got his work cut out if he's going to get rid of that lot by lunchtime.'

Aled was looking on the bright side. 'We'll get overtime, won't we, sir?'

'I've never been to an exorcism,' observed Gemma. 'I think it'll be interesting.'

'No, it won't,' said Aled. 'It'll be dead boring. Nothing is likely to happen apart from a lot of bells and smells. Wasting police time, if you ask me.'

* * *

It was late on Saturday evening before Jack and Corrie were home together long enough to chat and share a glass of wine. Talk of exorcism had reminded Jack he was distracted by the case of Summer Johnson. She was clearly more deserving of exorcism than the busybodies of Kings Richington, who were simply seeking to get maximum value from their council tax.

Jack sighed. 'How could someone so young be so intrinsically evil, Corrie? I don't understand. When we first interviewed her, with that Lilith woman there, she sounded so plausible. I honestly believed that men had broken in and killed her grandparents while she hid in the wardrobe. You know how long I've been a copper. How come I didn't realize it was a pack of lies?'

'That's exactly the point, sweetheart — you're a copper, not a psychiatrist. You're not trained to deal with deeply disturbed minds, only criminal ones. You have to leave inner demons to the experts.'

'Once we got her back to the station, away from the malevolent influence of that blasted Foundation, she told us what really happened, so now we can get her the help she undoubtedly needs. That place is evil, Corrie. I have a really bad feeling about it. Promise me you won't go there again. Not until we've sorted it out.'

'Funny you should feel like that. Cynthia and I thought just the opposite. We felt it had a peaceful, calm ambience. Carlene agrees with you, though. She's had some of the members in the bistro and her view was that the place is "seriously random". She called it a "home for loony tunes".'

'If that's all it is, that's fine, but my copper's nose tells me there'll be more deaths before this is over.' Jack topped up their glasses and Corrie got the impression he had more to get off his chest. It could be a long evening. 'The worthy folk of Kings Richington — well, most of them — have got a serious case of the heebie-jeebies. Since the bodies of Sir Bixby Carrington and Councillor Hughes-Jones turned up in that same location on the tomb, within weeks of each other, they've been demanding answers. Apparently, the editor of the *Echo* has encouraged the view that since the police don't seem able to act, there should be an exorcism to "cleanse the area of evil spirits".'

Corrie snorted in disgust. 'What poppycock! It's just a way to boost the circulation.'

'I know, but people are gullible. According to Garwood, they're split into two camps — the bored ones who want a bit of excitement and the ones who are scared the ghoulies and ghosties are going to get them. As taxpayers, they reckon the police should be protecting them in any way possible.'

'Who's going to perform this exorcism? It has to be an ordained priest, doesn't it?'

'The mayor has asked Father Bartholomew.'

'Surely not the Father Bartholomew who lives in one of the almshouses?' Corrie was astounded.

'That's him. Why?'

'Jack, he's ninety if he's a day. Carlene takes him snacks from Corrie's Kitchen.'

'I expect he can still remember all the stuff he has to recite. It's not as if it matters one way or the other. It's the process that's important. Puts everyone's minds at rest.'

'If you say so, darling. I hope they're bunging the old bloke a few quid for turning out.' She held out her glass. 'Is there anymore wine in that bottle?'

* * *

Despite the police asking people not to crowd the clearing, there was a large turnout, eager to witness Father Bartholomew's performance. He came well prepared with specific prayers according to the rubrics of the rite — liturgical instructions explaining what he must do. He started well, walking the perimeter of the clearing in a surplice and a purple stole and swinging a burning thurible. It contained aromatic incense to symbolize the prayers of the faithful, rising like smoke to heaven.

Next, he sprinkled holy water on the slab of the tomb, which was no longer black, having been thoroughly scrubbed of the paint and the remains of the chalk pentacle. Once he had prepared the ground with icons and sacramentals, he made the sign of the cross several times over the tomb.

'He's good, isn't he?' whispered Gemma. She glanced sideways at Aled. 'That's a posh suit you're wearing. I can't even smell the mothballs.'

Aled grinned. 'Thought I'd better show some respect, it being Sunday and all. Chapel upbringing, isn't it? He's a nice old bloke, Father Bartholomew. Let's hope it isn't too much for him. I understand this type of thing can take a lot out of a priest. What do you think, sir?' he asked Jack. 'Is this going to satisfy the troubled citizens of Kings Richington?'

Jack frowned. 'I think superstition ought not to be confused with religion, however much people believe they're the same. In my opinion, this whole debacle is superstition gone mad.'

In a loud voice that belied his age, Father Bartholomew appealed first to the saints, then in Jesus's name he called upon any demons to 'yield to God' and 'depart this place'. Some half an hour later, once he was convinced the exorcism had worked, he said prayers to prevent demons and evil spirits from returning. Finally, he climbed up onto the tomb with the assistance of a stepladder and the arm of a burly police constable. He threw his arms wide and proclaimed '*Vade retro Satana*' — 'Step back, Satan.' Then he gasped, clutched his chest, fell headlong off the tomb and lay motionless on the grass.

There were horrified screams from the crowd. An ambulance was called, but it was too late. Father Bartholomew had been dead before he hit the ground.

CHAPTER FOURTEEN

'Well, that's just bloody wonderful!' Garwood was furious. 'Instead of solving the problem, the exorcism has made it a damn sight worse.' He paced up and down the incident room, where a photo of Father Bartholomew's dead body had joined the others on the whiteboard. He turned on Jack. 'How did you let this happen, Dawes? Now all the crackpots who believe the forest is possessed by demons will be convinced they're right. The editor of the *Echo* will have a field day. Of course, he had one of his reporters and a photographer in the crowd. I can just imagine the lurid headlines.'

Jack tried to pacify him. 'Father Bartholomew was elderly, sir. Even the *Echo* will have to concede that it was simply too much for the poor old gentleman.'

Garwood was far from reassured. 'Do you imagine for a single moment that the kind of people who read the *Echo* will believe it? This is the most excitement some of them have had in years. First the suspicious deaths of two well-known Richington residents, left slaughtered on a tomb, then the priest trying to exorcize the place drops dead. Conspiracy theories don't even come close. Any kind of rational explanation will be rejected as a police cover-up.' He ran anxious fingers through what was left of his hair. 'Sir Barnaby has hinted that there'll be an enquiry and mark my words, Dawes, this time you won't come out of it smelling of roses.' He strode back to his office, munching indigestion tablets.

The commander, Sir Barnaby Featherstonehaugh (pronounced Fanshaw) was prickly on a good day. Bugsy always reckoned it was because his nickname at public school had been 'Fanny'. Exposure to such mortification at an early age could, according to Bugsy, have resulted in stress from being unable to choke the living shit out of the bastards responsible. However, Sir Barnaby had suggested on several occasions that it was time Jack Dawes was promoted to chief inspector. Garwood had strenuously resisted this on the basis that without Jack, his clear-up rate would plummet.

'That went well,' commented Bugsy, dryly. 'The old man has really got his knickers in a twist.'

Jack chose to be magnanimous. 'He's still upset by the death of his old friend.'

'I don't see why the exorcism was our fault,' complained Gemma. 'It was the mayor who gave in to public pressure and arranged the whole thing.'

* * *

Charlie Updike had been the *Echo* reporter in the crowd that morning and he was responsible for the headline the next day.

Priest dies performing exorcism while helpless police look on. Did the power of evil overcome the power of law and order?

From the point of view of lowering the temperature of the readers, it wasn't helpful. The editor, however, was delighted with Charlie's copy and printed it in full on the front page. There was a great deal of criticism of the management of the exorcism. Questions were asked about the failure of the police to carry out the appropriate risk assessments, and what happened to their duty of care for the elderly priest? Worse, however, was the suggestion that demons had disapproved of the whole shebang and had taken their revenge.

'What kind of numpties believe this rubbish?' Bugsy threw down the paper in disgust.

'They probably don't,' said Jack. 'Maybe they're just searching for a different belief system from the one they no longer trust, like Professor MacDuff suggested.'

The phone rang. Gemma answered it. It was the desk sergeant. 'There's a Professor MacDuff to see Inspector Dawes.' It was almost as if they had conjured him up.

'*Arswydus*,' muttered Aled.

'That's enough of that, young Taffy,' admonished Bugsy. 'Don't you start with your Celtic spooks. It's creepy enough in English.'

The professor was introduced to the rest of the team and offered coffee and biscuits before Jack asked him the purpose of his visit.

'When we last met, Inspector, you asked me whether there was any substance to the belief in demons, among modern academics. If you recall, I told you that servants of the devil could, either on their own or with the devil acting through them, harm or illicitly influence other people by occult. I believe that's what happened on Sunday in Richington Forest.'

'Professor, are you seriously telling us that Father Bartholomew was killed by demons who were resentful of his attempt to banish them?' asked Gemma.

'What I'm saying is that an exorcism is a confrontation and not simply a prayer. Once it has begun, it has to finish, no matter how long it takes. If the exorcist stops the rite, then the demon will pursue him, which is why it's so essential that the process is finished.'

'But I thought Father Bartholomew did complete the exorcism,' said Bugsy. 'Wasn't it that bit at the end when he stood on the tomb and drove out Satan?'

'It can sometimes take days, even weeks to expel a deeply entrenched demon. But where I think the problem lies is in the choice of cleric. His faith in God was resolute, but like you, Sergeant, Father Bartholomew wasn't totally convinced that the demons he had been called upon to exorcize even existed. Once they sensed this, he was a dead man.'

* * *

'Professor MacDuff is mad as a box of frogs. I did warn you, Inspector.' Dr Hardacre was conducting the post-mortem on Father Bartholomew in the presence of Jack, Bugsy and Aled. 'Well, here we are again, gentlemen. It's becoming a full-time job working with you.' She indicated the fifth corpse provided by the MIT in as many weeks. 'This poor old sausage died of natural causes — no more, no less.'

'No indication of anything suspicious before the conking-out process, Doc?' asked Bugsy.

'Like what? He was ninety-four with a weak heart. The "conking-out process", as you so eloquently put it, was an acute myocardial infarction. I don't know what you were thinking, asking him to perform such antics on a tomb at his age.'

'I wish people would stop blaming the police,' complained Jack. 'We didn't organize this farce. We were there simply to try and prevent any trouble.'

Dr Hardacre raised her bushy eyebrows. 'An unkind person might say you should have tried harder.'

* * *

Solomon was ecstatic to the point of hysteria. He burst into the Lodge, where Lilith and Urbain were counting the money they'd taken that week. 'Now do you believe me?' He almost skipped around the desk where they were working, the girdle around his long, striped robes swinging as he went. 'Astaroth soon put a stop to that old charlatan. The Grand Duke of Hell showed him who ranks highest in the chaos of time and space.'

Urbain was unimpressed. 'Sit down, Sol, or you'll give yourself a heart attack like the poor old priest.'

Solomon ignored him and continued to rejoice. 'Of course, Father Bartholomew was a bad choice, right from the start, but the non-believers wouldn't have had the sense to know it.'

'Why was he a bad choice, Solomon?' Lilith humoured him, hoping he would calm down. If anything, it renewed his enthusiasm.

'*Saint* Bartholomew was Astaroth's adversary, and could allegedly protect people against Astaroth because he had resisted his temptations. People believed Astaroth could be thwarted by calling upon Saint Bartholomew for help. Because the old priest was called Bartholomew, Astaroth was able to manipulate the ritual and destroy him.' Solomon inhaled deeply. 'Did you notice his powerful stench and stinking breath? It was proof, if any were needed, that Astaroth was among us.' He swept out, chanting unintelligible incantations.

Urbain frowned. 'It's no good, Lilith. You need to have Solomon looked at — he's barking.'

Lilith was starting to think Urbain was right. Solomon had gone right over the edge. 'What was all that about a stench?'

Urbain was fastidious when it came to smells. 'It probably came from that disgusting, striped dressing-gown-thing that he insists on wearing. He looks like a bloody deckchair. I doubt it's been washed for months. His personal hygiene could do with some attention, too. The stinking breath, if there was one, would have been coming from Solomon, not Astaroth.'

CHAPTER FIFTEEN

Tuesday had been a sunny summer's day, so it was at least eleven o'clock before it was properly dark. Charlie put on black jeans and a black hoodie and crept out of his room in the Foundation House. Outside, he switched on his pencil torch and made for the Lodge. He was pretty sure that was where he would find what he was looking for. Since the editor of the *Echo* had assigned him to this job, Charlie had become more and more convinced that here was a story big enough to make the nationals. He had already had his byline on the front page of the *Echo* for his report on the exorcism. The big story behind the commune could kick-start his whole career.

It had all begun when a drinking buddy of the editor had claimed he'd seen and heard what he called 'obscene goings-on' late one night on his way home from the Richington Arms. He agreed that he'd had rather more than a half of shandy, but all the same, after the two dead bodies turned up, it had spooked him enough not to want to go back. He claimed to have seen shadowy figures in hooded robes making for the gates of the old convent. The editor had made the connection to the Foundation of the Free Spirit and told Charlie to get in there and see what he could find out. Obscene goings-on were exactly what kept readers of the *Echo* buying the paper or following it online.

In the meantime, he had been content to run with the Beast of Richington Forest story, to hold the public's interest. Then the missing granddaughter of the murdered pensioners had turned up, also living inside the Foundation House. Add to that the dramatic end to the public exorcism and it was all coming together nicely.

Charlie had expected the Lodge to be locked, so he had come prepared with various gadgets to unlock it — a skill he had learned during a somewhat chequered adolescence. It took him no more than four minutes to get in. He left the door on the latch for a quick getaway, should it be necessary. A quick tour of the small rooms confirmed that the office was the most likely place where he would find what he was looking for. He was careful not to shine his torch where it might be spotted from outside. Even with his ability to think on his feet in a tight corner, he would have had trouble explaining what he was doing, snooping late at night in a building with 'No Entry' signs on the door.

He decided to start with the laptop on the desk. Gone were the days when what you were looking for was in a filing cabinet and all you had to do was unlock it and photograph the contents. He could open the laptop easily enough but the files he wanted were, of course, password-protected. They had cryptic names — Astaroth, Aces High, Greenhouse Gas and other totally unconnected titles. His lock-cracking skills were no use with that. He tried a few random words but with no success. Eventually, he decided to copy everything onto the memory stick he'd brought with him. The Echo's tech team would be able to break the passwords.

There was a noise outside. Someone was coming in. Hastily, he leaped up from the desk, turned off his torch and hid behind the door. It opened slowly. He couldn't see who it was but he recognized the perfume — Georgia. As she crept in and moved towards the desk, he slipped in stealthily behind her. 'Hello, Georgia. Fancy meeting you here.'

She gasped out loud and jumped a good metre backwards, bashing her knee on the desk. 'Bloody hell, Charlie! You scared the life out of me.'

He grinned. 'Weren't you suspicious when you found the door open?'

'No, I just thought they'd forgotten about it. Did you pick the lock?'

'Yep. One of the many skills that keeps me in a job.'

'And what is that job? Are you a burglar or a safe-cracker?' she asked, only half joking. She wouldn't have been at all surprised either way. There was a substantial-looking safe in the corner of the room. She pointed. 'Can you break into that?'

It was the first thing he'd looked at when he arrived. 'No, 'fraid not. that's one of the heavy-duty, fireproof, digital jobs. Top of the range. Anyway, all I'm looking to pinch is information.'

'Me too. I see you've found the laptop. I guess there'll be useful stuff on there.'

'Only if we can crack the passwords. I was planning to load it all onto a memory stick and take it away.'

'Good idea.' She produced her own from a lanyard around her neck.

'Give it to me and I'll do it for you,' offered Charlie.

She handed it over and he put it into the laptop. After several minutes, he gave it back to her and she hung it around her neck. He took her elbow. 'I think we'd better get out of here before someone catches us.'

'Can you lock the door again?' she asked.

He grinned. 'Of course. Let's go.'

* * *

Next morning, Charlie was eager to get his memory stick to the editor as soon as possible. He felt sure there would be enough juicy revelations on it to make him a lot of money. He decided to skip breakfast but dropped into the refectory to have a quick coffee. The other members of the commune were tucking into eggs, bacon and homemade bread, except for Len and Trottie, who were nibbling at their usual vegan granola bars like a couple of hamsters. Come to think of it, Charlie reckoned granola bars looked like something made from the stuff at the bottom of a hamster cage. He smiled to himself, remembering seeing the couple in Chez Carlene chomping on rare steak. He was saving that piece of information for when it would cause them the most embarrassment — like when they were being particularly sanctimonious. He had no idea why they were pretending to be something they weren't, but it was certain to be fishy, like most of the other cult members. Gideon had been and gone, and Mae was feeding Goliath sausages from her plate.

'Really, Charlie,' clucked Harriet, 'you should eat something. It isn't good for young people to skip breakfast, especially as you seem to use so much energy.'

He gave her a quick peck on the cheek. 'Thanks, Harriet, my old darling, but I'm in a bit of a hurry today.' Whatever scandalous strife was going on, Charlie didn't believe that she had any part in it.

Lilith looked up from her yogurt. 'Where are you off to, Charlie?' The yogurt, and the subsequent cheese, were Howard and Harriet's latest enterprise. They had acquired a couple of Belgian goats, the same breed that the nuns had brought with them from Brussels. They were proving extremely successful and their milk was a nourishing addition to the commune's diet.

Charlie put a finger to the side of his nose. 'Oh, you know, Lilith — places to go, people to see.' He gulped down the coffee that she had poured for him. 'See you guys later.'

He decided to call ahead to the editorial office, so they could have the necessary expertise available to crack the passwords on the files as soon as he got there. It was always the first bloke to get the scoop that earned the big money, so there was no time to lose. Added to which, he was sure that Georgia was a rival, although she wouldn't admit it. After all, what else would she be doing in a dump like this, if she wasn't a top-class journo from the nationals, looking for the same story as him? He smiled to himself. Well, she wouldn't get very far with what he had downloaded to her memory stick. Served her right for trying to beat him to it. He went back to his room to put on his leathers and collect his crash helmet.

Outside, he kick-started the Harley and revved it a few times, just to listen to the throaty roar. He was feeling good — very good. The sun was out, but he thought he could see a rainbow — all the colours of the spectrum, spinning in his head. The world was beautiful, he decided. A quick ride down to the shed to collect his phone and the vital memory stick, from where he'd hidden it in a gardening glove, then he'd be away. With any luck, he'd be out of here for good by the end of the week.

The bike was going like a dream. He wound up the throttle and sped off — nought to sixty in four seconds. Soon he was doing seventy, eighty, ninety. As he flashed past the lake, he saw swirling, multicoloured patterns, like a spectrum, floating on the surface. The twelve-foot perimeter wall was approaching fast. He laughed out loud. He could fly. His bike was a plane. He pulled back on the handlebars, ready to take off and soar over the wall.

Two council workers, mowing the grass outside the convent, heard the deafening crash and saw Charlie's body fly over the wall. He hit the ground and bounced several yards before coming to a juddering halt. They rushed to help, dialling the emergency services as they ran. But when they reached him, the shredded leathers and horrific injuries confirmed what they feared — it was too late. They stood, helpless, breathing in the smell of burning rubber and petrol drifting over the wall. Ambulance sirens sounded in the distance.

* * *

The post-mortem was brief. Dr Hardacre looked sombre as she always did, but more so in the case of a young person, dead before his time. Miss Catwater was in attendance, as were Inspector Dawes, Sergeant Malone and DCs Williams and Fox.

'The deceased is a well-nourished young man of around twenty-five, who died attempting to fly his motorcycle over a wall. I ran a tox screen and it showed he had a considerable amount of lysergic acid diethylamide in his system. In my opinion, he had ingested it approximately twenty minutes before his death. This would have considerably impaired his judgement and not least his ability to ride a motorcycle.'

'Did he have a history of drug taking, Doc?' asked Bugsy.

'I found no traces apart from the one large dose he swallowed before death. He was otherwise fit and healthy. No other addictions or evidence of alcohol or tobacco.' She looked at Jack. 'This is one for you, Inspector. You need to find out why this happened — if only for the poor lad's relatives.'

Outside, nobody spoke until Aled observed, grimly, 'Saint Columbanus of the Motorbikes wasn't much help to him, was he?'

CHAPTER SIXTEEN

'Enough!' declared Dawes. He was standing in front of the whiteboard, which now bore pictures of Charlie Updike and Father Bartholomew alongside the gruesome photos of Sir Bixby Carrington and Councillor Mrs Hughes-Jones. 'We've done enough pussyfooting around this blasted commune. We've got four bodies now, all with enough of a connection to be more than coincidental.'

The room was silent. The team had rarely seen the inspector so fired up. This was not the time for quips or smart-arsed remarks. They listened, ready to spring into action as soon as he asked them.

He paced up and down. 'Warrant or no warrant — we're going to turn that place inside out. It's time to ask some serious questions and demand serious answers.'

'Guv,' ventured Malone, the only one brave enough to speak. 'Won't there be accusations of victimization and heavy-handed police tactics? Some might say it's oppression of a minority — a few gentle souls who just want to live an alternative lifestyle.'

'Some might say that, Sergeant, but *I* say to hell with the PC brigade! It isn't acceptable to hinder a police enquiry with their *ad hominem* attacks simply because they wouldn't survive in a debate using plain facts and logic. People have died and it's our job to find out why — and who did it.' He turned back to the troops. 'You all know about the bodies of two of Kings Richington's well-known citizens, who ended up ripped open and left in the forest. Most of you were present when Father Bartholomew died.' He pointed at the mangled body of Charlie Updike. 'Now we have this young man, a journalist on the *Echo*, who, according to Doctor Hardacre, was so full of fairy dust he thought he could fly his motorbike over a twelve-foot wall. He had no history of drug abuse and no previous form — not even a parking ticket. It's my theory that he discovered something shocking that would make a good story, something big enough to upset some important people. He may even have been encouraged to join the commune by the editor, for that very reason. You interviewed the bloke, Gemma. What was his account?'

'The editor flatly denied any responsibility, sir — said that Updike was an independent journalist, self-employed, and did it all on his own initiative.'

Dawes wasn't surprised. 'If the lad had come to us with his story, instead of trying to sell it, he might still be alive. Someone in that commune knew what he'd found out and had to put a stop to it, before he had a chance to publish.'

It was at this point that Jack noticed Bugsy jabbing an urgent thumb over his shoulder, towards the back of the room. Chief Superintendent Garwood had slipped in unnoticed. *No doubt*, thought Jack, *he's totting up how much all this proposed activity is going to cost and the possible impact on his next promotion*. This time, Jack intended to stand his ground. 'Sir, before you say anything, I really think this is too important to allow considerations such as . . .'

Garwood silenced him with a raised hand. He was looking at the photograph of his old and once dear friend, now dead and mutilated. 'Do it, Dawes. I'll back you.' He turned and left the room.

'Blimey!' said Bugsy.

The room was hushed for a few moments.

'OK, team,' Jack continued. 'Before we go in mob-handed and rattle their cages, let's look at what we've got to hit them with. We need to get our ducks in a row first.'

'Are we going to take Lilith and her two goons in for questioning, guv?' asked Bugsy.

'No, I don't think so — not at this stage. I think we'll find out more if we grill them in situ. They'll be aware of our officers searching the place, and if we're right about their involvement, they'll be unnerved about what we're finding and crack.' Jack pointed at the additional items written on the board. 'Firstly, let's consider Sir Bixby Carrington. The lab has confirmed that the water in his stomach, and the fish scales and water lily petals, match the sample of water Gemma took from the lake, so we can be pretty sure that's where he drowned. Time of death was between midnight on Friday and four o'clock the next morning.'

'We know how, when and where he died.' Aled was tapping away on his computer. 'But not why.'

'Correct. We don't yet know what he was doing in the convent grounds that night, with a considerable amount of drink and drugs in his system. We know he had alcohol and gambling addictions, but why the LSD? The same drug that was responsible for Charlie Updike's accident, which will probably turn out to be murder. And after Carrington drowned, why did someone fish him out of the lake, take his body into the forest, mutilate it so it looked like an animal attack and leave him naked on the tomb? We want answers to those questions and I'm pretty certain the people running this place will have them.'

'Incidentally, the chief super has asked if we could keep an eye out for his Rolex. It was an anniversary present and important to his widow.' Garwood had emailed Bugsy the memo.

Jack pointed at the photo of Councillor Hughes-Jones. 'There are all kinds of question marks over this lady, not least the odd timings and personal nature of the DNA deposits on the tomb. This is a seemingly respectable councillor with aspirations of being the next mayor of Kings Richington.'

A young constable at the front put up his hand. 'How about this for a possible scenario, sir? The councillor and her hubby have been married nearly twenty years and action in the bedroom department has got a bit stale. She decides to spice things up by taking Mr Hughes-Jones into the woods, where they take all their clothes off and have it away on the tomb. This works well, so a couple of weeks later, they decide to do it again. The post-mortem showed she died from a whack on the head, but she wasn't hit with an object. Doctor Hardacre says the blunt force trauma was caused by falling on a stone edge and cracking her skull. What if she was on top, but in the heat of the . . . er . . . moment, she fell and split her head open on the edge of Saint Columbanus's tomb? Mr Hughes-Jones is a company director and he's embarrassed so he does the business with the rake so it looks like a copycat of Sir Bixby's death. He gathers up her clothes and goes home. That would explain the DNA samples spaced a couple of weeks apart, wouldn't it?'

'Nice try, son, but no cigar,' said Bugsy. 'For a start, I don't think old Paul could leave her there like that — he loved her. His story is that she went out late that night on council business and I think that's the truth, only whatever the business was, it got her killed. Added to which, the fragments in her head come from a different type of stone than the limestone tomb.'

'Do we have any clues as to where she fell?' asked Gemma.

Jack pursed his lips. 'Not officially, but I have a pretty good idea that it happened on the chancel steps in the convent chapel. They've been thoroughly washed recently, but the rest of the chapel hasn't been cleaned for ages. Even with washing, Forensics can usually find minute traces of blood if there are any to be found. Doctor Hardacre believes she can match the fragments of stone in the wound, once we've found the crime scene.'

'How did we know the chancel steps had been washed, sir?' asked Aled. 'I didn't think we looked inside the chapel when we were there.'

'We didn't, Aled. I received the information from an outside source. The same source reported finding a very large cannabis farm. That's something else for the charge sheet. Finally, there's Charlie Updike, unable to tell us now what it was he found out. But he was a newshound — I can't believe he won't have left something behind. Right, you know what we have to do. Let's go.'

'What bit of PACE code of practice underpins our raid on this place, sir?' asked a fresh-faced constable, scribbling furiously in a notebook.

'It's Section Sixty-Nine of the Ways and Means Act, son,' replied Bugsy. 'If you can't nick 'em one way, nick 'em another.' He tapped the notebook. 'Don't write that down.'

* * *

Lilith, Urbain and Solomon were in the Lodge planning the next Black Mass. It was a lucrative part of their business and they tried to organize one every couple of months. The usual method was to put a message in the personal column of the *Echo*, coded in such a way that the faithful knew what it meant, but nobody who was likely to make trouble would understand it. Rather than scaring people off, the bodies found on the tomb had served to whet the appetites of the more bizarre demon enthusiasts. The failed exorcism that had resulted in the death of Father Bartholomew had fired up their enthusiasm even further.

Lilith glanced through the window from where she could just see the main gates, some distance away, and spotted the police convoy snaking up the long drive. No doubt they were coming to ask about Charlie Updike's death. It should never have happened within the convent estate — that was a regrettable mistake. No matter. She was ready with answers. She alerted Urbain and Solomon. 'Gentlemen, the storm clouds are gathering. Operation Cover-Up!'

The trio had rehearsed this routine until it went like clockwork. Now, as with many previous such emergencies,

Lilith gave the orders. She opened the safe and took out a strongbox. Together with her laptop, she handed it to Solomon.

'You know what to do with these. Be quick. There isn't much time.'

He objected. 'Lilith, that place is sacred to Astaroth. The Grand Duke of Hell won't tolerate your secular paraphernalia alongside his Satanic accoutrements. Mark my words, there will be repercussions.'

'Solomon, just do it! Or do you want to end up locked away for the rest of your life?'

He took the items and hurried away, muttering imprecations. Lilith produced an identical laptop from her desk drawer — one that the police could scroll through for as long as they wished and find nothing untoward. Nor would they find any information online, as she had it carefully concealed in a number of different accounts that could not be traced back to her. Not without the information on the other laptop.

'What about Len and Trottie's cannabis?' asked Urbain.

'Harvested yesterday and well on its way to be processed. There's only a slight lingering smell and the police can't arrest you for a smell.' She relocked the safe, knowing that very shortly the police would require her to unlock it again. It contained legitimate Foundation papers and a few documents relating to the convent's history. Suddenly she spotted Carrington's Rolex. There was no time to hide it safely.

'Urbain, put this on, quickly.' He took it and slipped it on his wrist just as Dawes and Malone came through the door.

'Inspector Dawes, Sergeant Malone, please come in and take a seat. I imagine you're here about Charlie? That poor boy — what a terrible accident. Why do young people gamble with their lives like that?' She gestured to Urbain, who was sitting on the opposite side of the desk. 'You remember Urbain, our liberal science guru, Inspector? Would you like me to ask Harriet to bring us some tea?' She picked up the intercom, but Dawes shook his head. 'No, thank you. I have a warrant to search these premises.' He placed it on the desk in front of her. Garwood had used his authority to rustle one up in a hurry. 'My officers are in the process of examining the entire estate and may require you to unlock any rooms or cupboards of interest.' *Which will be all of them*, he thought.

Lilith was a picture of calm and innocence. 'I see. Can you perhaps tell me what it is you're searching for? Maybe I could assist in some way.'

Like she's going to do that, thought Bugsy. 'Could we start by seeing your CCTV, madam?'

She smiled condescendingly. 'Bless you, Sergeant, we don't spy on our members. Most of them are here because their spirits have already been diminished by excessive surveillance in their previous life.'

'So you don't have any?' Bugsy reckoned it wasn't the members who didn't want to be observed. More likely it was the crooks running this place who didn't want anyone to see what they were up to.

'No, we most definitely do not.'

'Miss . . . er,' began Dawes.

She smiled. 'Please, just call me Lilith.'

'Lilith, what do you know about the death of Charlie Updike?'

'Only that it was a terrible accident. He hadn't been with us long, so we had no idea he took drugs. We don't encourage drug taking here. If members need to function in a different dimension, they join Rushil's yoga and meditation classes.'

'You already know that when he died, his system contained a large dose of LSD?' asked Dawes.

'That kind of news travels fast, Inspector. The Foundation of the Free Spirit may be a discrete community but we don't live in a vacuum.'

'The post-mortem showed he took it around twenty minutes before he died. Would you have any idea where he got it?' asked Dawes, eyeballing her.

She eyeballed him back. 'Where do any youngsters get drugs these days? It's a volatile market. All I can tell you for certain is that he didn't get it here.'

'Drugs are the cause of so many ruined lives, Inspector Dawes,' declared Urbain. 'We are totally against any kind of recreational substances.' Lilith half expected his nose to grow.

Jack pressed on. 'We know he was working as a journalist on the *Echo*. According to the editor, he was planning to do an exposé on this cult. If he was intending to report to the newspaper on the day he died, why was he travelling at speed in the opposite direction, instead of down the road into town?'

She shrugged. 'You'd have to ask him that — but, of course, you can't, can you? And I can't imagine what kind of exposé you think he was planning. There really isn't anything to expose.'

Jack nodded to Bugsy to take over the interrogation. A two-pronged attack always worked well.

'What do you know about the two bodies found in Richington Forest?'

'Only what we read in the *Echo*. They were attacked by some wild beast in the night. What a ghastly way to die.'

Bugsy leaned forward in his chair. 'But that isn't how they died, is it? We have forensic evidence that Sir Bixby Carrington drowned in your lake between midnight and four o'clock.'

She ignored Bugsy and looked straight at Jack. 'Where exactly are you going with this, Inspector? Are you trying to imply that the Foundation had something to do with that man's death? If so, I think I should ring the company solicitor before I answer any more of your questions.'

Before Jack could reply there was a tap on the door. Gemma Fox put her head round. 'Sarge, could I have a word, please?'

Lilith took advantage of the interruption to put her foot on a poker scorecard that had been dropped on the floor, in the hurry to conceal incriminating evidence. She kicked it under the table. Sloppy! Mistakes like that could cost dearly.

Outside, Gemma showed Bugsy a photo on her phone. 'Forensics have examined the chancel steps and they've found traces of blood, despite it being scrubbed with bleach. They've taken samples of the stone, and if Doctor Hardacre can match that and the blood to Mrs Hughes-Jones—'

'We'll have got 'em!' said Bugsy. 'Good work.'

Back inside the Lodge, Bugsy faced Lilith and Urbain with the information he had just acquired. 'So you see, madam, we can trace the death of both victims back here.'

Lilith stood her ground. 'If what you say can be proved and isn't just police scare tactics, it still doesn't prove the Foundation had any involvement in their deaths. We don't lock the gates. Anyone could stumble in during the night, possibly drunk and incapable, fall in the lake and drown. As for Councillor Hughes-Jones, I imagine a woman in her position must be under a lot of stress. Our chapel is a place of peace and contemplation. What's to say she didn't go for a walk to clear her head, wander in here and spend some time in the chapel, looking for tranquillity? She lost her footing on the chancel steps — no doubt well-worn from all those nuns traipsing up and down — then fell and banged her head. No, Sergeant, you don't have evidence of any crime that isn't circumstantial.' She made it sound a direct challenge.

You have to hand it to her, thought Bugsy, *she doesn't freak easily*. 'Why did you wash the steps?'

She raised her eyebrows. 'I wasn't aware that cleaning was against the law. It's possible whoever cleaned them saw the blood and assumed it belonged to some wounded animal — maybe even the Beast of Richington Forest. You should understand, Sergeant, many of our members are deeply religious and would not have wanted the chapel defiled in that way.'

Jack could feel the initiative slipping away. 'If what you say is true, how do you explain the bodies ending up in Richington Forest, naked and eviscerated?'

Lilith laughed out loud. 'I can't explain it, Inspector. But then, I don't have to, do I? That's your job.'

Finally, after more fruitless interrogation, with Lilith successfully stonewalling every question, the two detectives left her and went to interview the remaining members of the Foundation.

Lilith waited until they were out of earshot. 'Urbain, what happened to the claw and the wheelbarrow?'

'They're at the bottom of the lake, just as you instructed.'

She frowned. 'I guess that's the best we could do in an emergency. Let's hope Inspector "Clever Dick" Dawes doesn't decide to send in divers to drag it.'

CHAPTER SEVENTEEN

Outside, Aled, Gemma, Mitch and a dozen or so uniformed officers were systematically turning over the convent estate. It was a lengthy job. Howard and Harriet were keeping the goats and hens out of the way. Mae had shut Goliath in her room. Howard went into the gardening shed to get some gloves — it was easier to grasp the goats' horns, wearing gloves.

'Harriet, look.' He showed her what he'd found, hidden in one of the gloves. 'What do you suppose these are doing here?'

Harriet turned them over in her hand. 'That's somebody's mobile phone and that looks like one of those gadgets you plug into a computer.'

'Should I hand them over to one of the police officers?' he asked.

She thought about it. 'No, don't do that. I think they must have belonged to Charlie — I used to see him sneaking in there sometimes. They're private and should go to his next of kin. It's up to them to decide what to do with them.' She put them in the pocket of her dungarees.

* * *

Each time the police came close, Gideon disappeared into a different part of the woodland. He was so adept at making himself invisible, they barely noticed him. Georgia was in her room, waiting to be questioned. The police had asked for a list of all the Foundation members, so she guessed it was only a matter of time before they got around to her. Charlie's death had hit her hard. She'd liked him a lot, despite the suspicion that he was trouble. The general consensus in the Foundation House was that he'd taken drugs and lost control of his bike. She didn't believe that for a moment. She'd guessed from what he'd said when they were in the Lodge that he was a journalist. Now, she had an uneasy suspicion that he'd been killed to stop him writing about what he'd found.

She was trying to decide what to tell the detectives when it was her turn. Finally, she decided to tell them the truth — who she was and why she was there. Too many people had died. She'd hoped to have come closer to completing her mission, but events had escalated. With her information and their extensive resources, she guessed the police would get there much faster. She hadn't even looked at what Charlie had downloaded onto her memory stick when they were in the Lodge. There was no point as she wouldn't be able to crack the passwords and the police would already have found Charlie's stick. They would have experts who could hack in. She would hand hers over to the police when they came to question her and let them decide what to do with it.

* * *

Gemma and Aled searched Charlie's room for any clues to his death.

'He travelled light, this bloke.' Aled was looking through the one small bag that constituted Charlie's belongings.

'That's because he didn't intend to stay,' said Gemma. 'Just long enough to get what he believed would be the story of his career.' She was feeling in the pockets of his jackets.

'Where's his phone? We know he had another one, apart from the one that he handed in when he arrived. It was how he reported to the editor of the *Echo*.'

'It wasn't on what was left of his body when they scraped him off the grass,' observed Aled.

She cuffed him on the shoulder. 'Show a bit of respect. The poor sod's dead.'

'Yeah — sorry.'

'My guess is that he hid it somewhere on the convent estate,' decided Gemma.

'In that case, Uniform will find it. They're doing a fingertip search.'

But uniform didn't find it, nor did they find anything else of much use to the investigation.

* * *

Bugsy was scanning the list of cult members. He had a retentive memory for names, especially those who had been connected with any sort of police investigation.

'This name, guv — Georgia Delacour. It's ringing bells, but I don't know why. I'm pretty sure someone of that name was in the news some time back.'

'Get Clive to do some digging. If there's anything to find, he'll find it.'

Brief interrogation of the remaining cult members revealed little apart from the belief that most of them were 'away with the fairies', as Bugsy put it. Simple minds leading harmlessly simple lives. They were a varied bunch that included a reformed burglar, a couple of ex-politicians not currently on remand and the former butler of a minor royal. They had not yet spoken to Len and Trottie, who were in the refectory preparing their vegan lunch. As they came down the corridor, they could hear Len extolling the virtues of Trottie's Zucchini Noodles in Brazil Nut Alfredo.

'Eh lass, that looks reet gradely.'

'It does look appetizing,' conceded Harriet.

Trottie smiled. 'Brazil nuts have such a nice flavour and they give it a lovely creamy texture.' She popped one in her mouth just as the police officers came through the door. Startled, she inhaled sharply. Seconds later, she was clutching at her throat — choking and turning blue.

Len rushed to her side, forgetting their phony identities in his anxiety. 'Keep coughing, Millie, try to spit it out.' Millie shot him an exasperated look. She was gasping for breath and certainly would have spat it out if she could.

Jack tried to remember the emergency first aid training he'd received. He bent her forward and slapped her hard several times between the shoulder blades but to no avail.

'Stand back — I've got this. She needs the Heimlich manoeuvre.' Bugsy grabbed her around the middle, applying upward pressure to try to force the nut out. It didn't work. She was beginning to lose consciousness.

'You're the police!' sobbed Len. 'Can't you get an ambulance?' He was beside himself with fear. 'Don't let her die!'

'There's no time for an ambulance.' Gideon appeared as if from nowhere. In seconds, he had thrown off his scruffy fringed jacket and sunglasses. 'Clear this table.'

Howard and Harriet grabbed everything off the table, laid for lunch, and between them, Jack and Bugsy picked up the now limp Trottie and lay her on it.

'What are you going to do?' beseeched Len.

'Better you don't watch,' growled Gideon. 'Take him outside, somebody.' Expertly, his hands no longer shaking, Gideon pulled out the case containing a scalpel that he kept in his pocket — a reminder of his deep remorse. He made an incision in the front of Trottie's neck, opening a direct airway into her trachea. 'I need a tube of some kind.'

'Will this do?' Jack offered his police biro. 'It's cheap but it might do the job.'

'Fine. Take out the ink refill. It'll keep the opening clear until the ambulance gets here.'

By the time the ambulance arrived, Trottie was breathing again, albeit with a raspy whistling sound. A tearful Len went with her to the hospital after insisting on hugging Gideon, which he found both embarrassing and unnecessary.

'Blimey,' breathed Bugsy. 'I thought she was a goner. Gideon, mate, that was amazing, what you did there.'

Harriet was making a large pot of tea to calm everybody's nerves. A couple of the younger girls were close to tears. Jack remembered that before all the excitement had kicked off, they had come into the refectory to interview the remaining cult members.

'Gideon, might we have a word?'

They took their mugs of tea into the Foundation common room. 'You didn't learn that in the boy scouts,' said Bugsy, still full of admiration.

'No,' confessed Gideon. 'I used to be a surgeon.'

'So what are you doing here, hidden away in a commune?' asked Jack.

Gideon took a long slug of tea — the only drink he did take, now. 'A child died on the operating table. It was my fault.'

'That's a tragedy,' said Bugsy, 'but I dare say the best of surgeons must lose a few patients. No reason to pack it in with skills like yours.'

Gideon looked down at his feet, still in the suede moccasins that were part of his alter ego. 'Yes, but you see, Sergeant, I wasn't the best of surgeons. It was a perfectly straightforward procedure, but I botched it —I'd been drinking. I was struck off, quite rightly. It was a while ago now, but the demons never leave me. I can't sleep without seeing that little girl's face, pale and lifeless. I spend most nights walking around the convent grounds.'

Bugsy thought it seemed heartless to question the poor bloke now, but they had a job to do. 'Have you seen anything unusual during these nightly walks? People wandering about who shouldn't be here — who aren't members of the Foundation?'

'To be honest, Sergeant, I see very little apart from that child's face. I can tell you that the two lefties, Len and Trottie, are harmless fakes. They aren't working class and they're not vegans. I've seen them sneaking into the kitchen at midnight to make bacon sandwiches. His real name's Tristan and he calls her Millie — the names they use here are a rather silly joke based on Lenin and Trotsky, which I imagine they find amusing. I think they had some kind of scam going. I'm sure Lilith knew about it, so I guess it's nothing to do with the murders or she would have reported it, wouldn't she?'

Jack and Bugsy exchanged glances, each with the same thought — Corrie and Cynthia's cannabis farm. The shed that Corrie had described had been empty when it was searched but it still had the telltale smell. Not much the drug boys could do with just a smell, and Jack doubted that Lilith would admit she knew anything about it. He wondered how much her cut was.

'Anything else you can tell us, sir?' asked Bugsy.

Gideon hesitated. 'You'll probably think I was imagining things — or drunk. I swear I haven't touched a drop since that child died.'

'Tell us what you saw, please, sir. We need to find out who's responsible for these three deaths.'

'It's always late on a Friday night, every month or so. I've seen what look like monks in black hooded robes. Usually three of them. They creep silently through the gates and make their way up to the house. At first, I thought they were the ghosts of the original inhabitants of the convent and that I was going mad, Inspector, but I'm sure they were real.'

Jack was thinking that two of the hooded figures might have been Sir Bixby and Mrs Hughes-Jones, but what reason would they have to be sneaking up to the convent in the dark? Added to which, their deaths had occurred some time apart and there was no evidence that they had even known each other.

'You haven't spotted anybody else? A man down by the lake, possibly the worse for drink, or a lady of about forty, near the chapel?' asked Bugsy.

Gideon shook his head. 'No, I'm afraid not, Sergeant. I saw your detective constable collecting a sample of the lake water, but I haven't seen a man hanging about down there. You could ask Howard. I believe he fishes for trout sometimes.' He suddenly remembered something. 'I saw a couple of middle-aged ladies behaving very suspiciously. I think they were pretending to be members of Rushil's yoga class because they were wearing sports gear, but I suspect that was just a cover for something crooked. They were snooping around the chapel and the outbuildings as if they were looking for something to steal, but Goliath surprised them and they ran off. I'm pretty sure they were up to no good. Do you think they had anything to do with the murders you're investigating?'

'I doubt it, sir,' replied Jack. 'We know who the two ladies are and we have eliminated them from our enquiries, but thank you for your help.'

CHAPTER EIGHTEEN

Howard and Harriet were unable to tell them anything new. They were still upset about Charlie's death and now Trottie had nearly died, right there in front of them.

'It's almost as if there are wicked demons among us, causing all this mischief,' said Harriet.

'Makes you wonder what will happen next,' agreed Howard. He was still in two minds about whether they should hand over Charlie's phone and memory stick to the police, but Harriet had been adamant that his family should see them first.

'Try not to worry,' said Bugsy. 'We have our best officers on the case. Rest assured we shall get to the bottom of it.'

'Lilith has told everybody that the police believe the two people who were found in Richington Forest, torn apart by a wild animal, might have actually died here by accident, on the convent estate. That they were only attacked by animals afterwards,' said Howard.

'But if that were true, how would they have ended up in the forest?' asked Harriet.

Good question, thought Jack. *That was smart of Lilith. She told the members herself rather than let them find out from the police — a sure way to keep them on her side and allay any suspicions.*

There were two people on the list still to interview. One of them was Georgia Delacour.

'Do you know where we might find Georgia?' asked Jack.

'She's in her room, waiting to speak to you. I'll take you up there,' offered Harriet.

Before they reached her room, Bugsy's phone rang. It was Clive from the station. 'I've tracked down what you wanted to know about Georgia Delacour, Sarge. She's the Honourable Georgia Delacour, her father's a viscount.'

'Good man, Clive. Did you get to the bottom of the article that I must have read in the news?'

'That was about her younger brother, the Honourable Peregrine Delacour. He hanged himself. He was only sixteen.'

'Blimey! Poor kid. What were the circumstances?'

'It was never very clear. The coroner's verdict was suicide, mainly because the deceased left a note. I had trouble finding it but I pulled a few strings. It said — and I quote — *"My death is an escape from the hypocrisies and persecution of this fake world. I'm going to follow Him, the one and only Lord."*'

'And that was it?'

'Yes, Sarge. They never came to a conclusion about who he meant by "the one and only Lord" except that it wasn't God or Christ. He was vociferously atheist, even at sixteen. The family weren't aware of any persecution, either.'

'Was he being bullied at school or on social media? There's a lot of it about, so I'm told.'

'It's a possibility, I guess. He ran away from a top boarding school to join a New Age cult, somewhere in Hampshire.'

'Now, that is interesting,' said Bugsy. 'Do we have a name for this cult?'

'Yep. They called themselves the Followers of the Enlightened Mind.'

'Are they still operating?'

'Nope. After the lad died and the police and the press started asking questions, they just vanished. Closed everything down and hopped it. I couldn't find any trace of bank records, personnel, registered business accounts — nothing. It was a clean exit. Most unusual not to leave anything behind, but they obviously knew what they were doing.'

'I dare say that's because they'd done it before. Thanks, son. Good work.'

'One more thing, Sarge. We ran all the fingerprints of the cult members through the database. The ones belonging to Mae came up with a different name — Verity Hargreaves.'

Bloody hell, thought Bugsy. *This place is full of people pretending to be someone else.* 'Has she got form?'

'Not exactly. She's on the witness protection programme. It's a closely guarded secret. I had to crack a few security screens before I could find it. Probably totally illegal.'

'Don't worry, son. I shan't tell anybody.' By the time Bugsy joined Jack in Georgia's room, she was telling him about her father, the viscount, and how he had taken the suicide of his only son rather badly.

'He loved Perry very much — more so since our mother died. He loved us both, but Perry was special — clever, funny, charming, handsome, he had everything to live for. Then he got mixed up with a cult.'

'Like this one?' probed Jack.

'Exactly like this one, Inspector.'

'And that's why you're here?' suggested Bugsy. 'You suspect it might be the same set-up under a different name?'

'I'm sure it is — but so far I haven't been able to prove anything. The coroner said Perry committed suicide because he was depressed, and after that, the police wouldn't do anything. But I don't believe it and neither does my father. His health has seriously declined since Perry's death. I was hoping if I could find out why, it might offer him a little comfort. I joined without giving them my surname so they wouldn't associate me with my brother. There are some good folk here, Inspector, but the atmosphere is toxic. I'm pretty certain they got rid of Charlie because he was getting too close to something evil.'

'How close?' asked Jack.

'He got as far as breaking into the Lodge where Lilith and her two partners in crime keep all the confidential stuff. We couldn't break the security, so he copied the files on her laptop. I believe, now, that's where he was going when he crashed the bike. He would expect the editor of the *Echo* to know someone who could hack in. Did you find his memory stick? I bet there's a lot of incriminating evidence on it.'

Jack and Bugsy exchanged glances. 'No, we didn't, Miss . . . er . . . Your Honourable,' said Bugsy. 'We didn't find his phone, either.'

She beamed. 'That's OK, Charlie copied the files onto my stick as well.' She took it from the chain around her neck. 'I haven't looked at it yet. I was waiting for an opportunity to give it to the police. You'll have an expert who can crack the passwords?'

'Absolutely. If we email it to the station, they can get started on it straight away.'

Georgia plugged the stick into her laptop, tapped a few keys then looked bewildered. 'I don't understand. It's blank. Charlie copied the same files onto my stick.'

'Did you actually see him do it?' asked Jack.

'Well, I thought I did.'

'It seems to me, miss, that Charlie Updike thought you might be a rival journalist and he wanted first dibs on the story.'

'Oh no.' She was crestfallen. 'I thought I had evidence about this cult and what they did to my brother. Now we'll never know.'

'Don't you believe it,' said Bugsy. 'DI Dawes and I are on the case now and we'll find out what's going on here — one way or another.'

But in Bugsy's own terminology, they were 'pissing in the wind'. Lilith had provided credible, if convenient, answers to all their questions and they still didn't have enough evidence for an arrest. If they went in now, without a solid case, a good barrister would make mincemeat of the Crown Prosecution. The cult would do a disappearing act and start up again somewhere else.

They found Mae exercising Goliath in the extensive grounds. She knew the police were speaking to everyone and guessed it was her turn. As soon as the dog saw Jack and Bugsy approaching, he came galloping across to welcome them, gaining speed with every stride. Jack sidestepped smartly, but Goliath caught Bugsy full in the chest. He keeled over backwards, winded.

Mae was mortified. 'Gollie, let the gentleman get up. He's a police officer.' She hauled him off.

Bugsy clambered to his feet, wheezing. 'Are you sure that animal's safe, madam? Shouldn't he be wearing a muzzle?' Even as he suggested it, Bugsy doubted they made muzzles that big.

Mae chuckled. 'Well, he hasn't eaten anybody yet.'

Jack steered her to a rustic bench and they sat down. 'It's Miss Verity Hargreaves, I believe.'

'Aah.' Her face fell. 'Of course, Inspector. You'll have traced me from my fingerprints. I did think that would be the case when the young constable took them.'

'We know you're on the witness protection programme, but we don't have any details. Maybe you could fill us in.'

She shrugged. 'It was a case of being in the wrong place at the wrong time. I had been rehearsing with the RPO — I was principal flute. We were doing *Daphnis et Chloé*, if I remember correctly. It's the flautist's pièce de résistance. On my way home — I was driving back to my flat in the city — I was unlucky enough to witness a gang shooting. It was a turf war of the most violent nature. If I'd had any sense, I would have carried on driving and forgotten what I saw, but my conscience wouldn't let me do that. Anyway, the outcome was that I gave evidence in a gangland prosecution and helped put away some notorious criminals. The police rehoused me under a covert name, and for a while, it was a closely guarded secret. But someone involved in the witness protection scheme was bribed and the gang members found me. The police said my life was in danger, that the criminals wouldn't think twice about killing me. Obviously, it put an end to my career as a flautist. I bought a camper van, adopted a big dog and went on the road. That was until I discovered the Foundation of the Free Spirit. It seemed an ideal place to remain anonymous. And there you have it, officers. I'm "Barmy Mae" who plays the flute and wears flowers in her hat.'

'I think you're a very brave woman, Miss Hargreaves,' said Jack. 'You can rest assured that your secret is safe with us.'

She looked thoughtful. 'It might just be me being fanciful, Inspector, but I sense that several of the members here are like me, hiding from their personal demons. The toxic trio running the Foundation are exploiting them. Now they're saying that Charlie died because he took drugs. I don't believe that — not for a moment. There's evil at work here and you need to get to the bottom of it. If I can assist in any way, I will.' She smiled, wryly. 'There I go again, sticking my neck out.'

There's that word again — 'toxic', thought Jack. *Two intelligent women of different ages and backgrounds, each with the same description.* He had to crack this case, whatever it took.

CHAPTER NINETEEN

When Jack arrived home, Corrie could tell from his face that the raid hadn't produced the results he'd wanted. He sank down at the kitchen table with a glass of dark, robust Rioja and took a large, restorative mouthful. It brought back memories of a holiday they had spent together.

'The last time we had this wine, it was with grilled pigeon and white truffle.'

Corrie lifted a casserole dish from the oven. 'Well, tonight we're having slow-cooked lamb shanks. I never know when you'll be home while this investigation is ongoing, so grilled food is off the menu.' She looked at his tired expression. 'Bad day?'

He took another mouthful of wine while she lifted a lamb shank onto his plate. 'That blasted cult is rife with evil, and Bugsy and I keep assuring people that we're going to get to the bottom of it. The truth is, we've no proper evidence to support a strong case. It's all circumstantial and supposition.' He helped himself to creamed potatoes. 'We took that place apart, Corrie, and found bugger-all that we could use. Even the cannabis farm had gone. We questioned all the cult members and took their statements — half of them aren't who they say they are, though that isn't necessarily a crime.

It reinforced our view that it's the hub of some very nasty goings-on, but we can't prove anything. I keep going over and over it in my mind, in case we've missed something.'

'Sweetheart, you'll get there. You always do.'

'Yes, but when? Crime doesn't just stop and wait for the cops to catch up.'

She was racking her brains to think of some way she could help him. Brainstorming with Cynthia and Carlene usually worked. She would book a table at the bistro so they could eat while they hatched a plan.

* * *

Back at the station, morale was low. Before the raid, the team had been upbeat and optimistic about early arrests. Now it seemed they were back to square one.

'My problem,' offered Aled, 'is that most of the statements we took, apart from the three villains running the place, could easily have been the truth. On the other hand, they could all have been lying through their teeth.'

'Honesty can be as big a smokescreen as deceit, young Aled,' said Bugsy. 'That's another brick in the wall of your police education, son.'

Gemma was chewing her lip, trying to remember something that she had believed to be important at the time, but had slipped away from her in the confusion that had followed. It suddenly came to her.

'Sarge, do you remember telling us that the chief super wanted us to keep a lookout for Sir Bixby Carrington's Rolex when we searched the Foundation? It had been an anniversary present from his wife and important to her.'

'Yep, he sent me a memo. She thought he might have pawned it or used it to pay his gambling debts. Never found it, though.'

'We might have. When you and the inspector were in the Lodge, questioning Lilith and Urbain, I put my head round the door and asked if I could have a word. You came outside and I told you about the blood that Forensics had found on the chancel steps.'

'I remember. The evil witch talked her way out of that one, too. What's your point, Gemma?'

'In the brief moments I was looking into the room, I spotted a Rolex.'

Jack was immediately alert. 'Where?'

'It was on Urbain's wrist. I only noticed it because I didn't think he looked rich enough to own a Rolex. Before you say anything, Sarge, I know that was judgemental of me and it isn't a good quality in a police officer.'

'Why didn't you say something at the time?' asked Jack.

'Sorry, sir. It went right out of my head. Then Aled and I went to search Charlie Updike's room and I didn't think of it until just now. Of course, I might be making the wrong judgement. Maybe he is well off enough to own one.'

Jack called across to the tech team. 'Clive, did you run Urbain's prints through the database?'

Clive checked. 'I don't think we ever had them, sir. Must have been missed when Uniform took all the others.'

'Damn,' said Jack. Yet another opportunity was slipping away.

'Yes, we do have them, sir,' said Gemma, redeeming herself. 'They'll be on the statement he signed. I remember he took the form and held on to it for some time while he read it. He said he wanted to make sure we weren't fitting him up for something.'

They found several clear prints on the statement form. Clive ran them through the database. 'Well, he isn't called Urbain, sir. His name's Bernard "Bernie" Bottle. He's served three longish stretches for dealing Class As, but nothing recent.'

Bugsy was doubtful. 'Either he's learned the error of his ways or he's learned how to stay under the drug squad's radar. My money's on the latter.'

'What about the Rolex?' asked Gemma.

'Might have been a good fake,' said Aled. 'Difficult to tell from a brief glance. On the other hand, if he's a drug dealer, he could probably afford a real one.'

'I'd be more impressed if he hadn't been caught so often,' said Bugsy.

'Did we check Lilith and Solomon's prints?' asked Jack, clutching at straws.

'Yes, sir. Nothing on the database. All the others are clean, too. Just the information we dug up on the Honourable Peregrine Delacour hanging himself. And I traced the news item about Doctor Gordon, alias Gideon, being struck off after operating on a child who died. He narrowly escaped a prison sentence.'

Jack reckoned a prison sentence would have been pointless. The bloke was already locked up in his own private prison — one he'd never be released from. 'Did Charlie Updike have a next of kin?'

'No, he was brought up in care. Left at sixteen and got a job as a cub reporter. Very keen to make the big time. He'd been doing quite well for himself — well enough to afford a Harley. Just needed that big scoop to sell to the nationals and look out, Rupert Murdoch.'

'Len and Trottie?'

'Couple of jokers. Tristan and Millie. Both from upper-class families.'

'We never got a chance to interview them properly after Millie nearly choked,' said Bugsy. 'I suppose the cannabis farm was their venture?'

'I don't think there's any doubt they were responsible, Sarge,' agreed Clive. 'When they were at university, they were at the forefront of demonstrations to legalize drugs. I found lots of pictures of them holding up placards on the front page of left-wing newspapers. Growing cannabis wasn't so much about needing the cash — it was more about raising two fingers to the establishment.'

'Where are they now?' asked Jack.

Clive scrolled down. 'Switzerland. Tristan took Millie there to recover as soon as she was released from hospital.'

'I thought we said nobody was to leave the area until we'd finished our enquiries,' said Bugsy.

'We did, Sarge,' confirmed Aled. 'Those two live in a world where you please yourself, never mind the law. They're mickey-takers.'

'They must have got Lilith's permission to use the building,' said Jack.

'Which means she was taking a hefty cut of the profits,' said Bugsy. 'Clive, son, are you sure your team of nerds can't find anything suspicious in the Foundation's accounts?'

'Sorry, Sarge. Clean as a whistle.'

Jack frowned. 'Lilith's too smart not to have a second set of accounts. There'll be another laptop somewhere with all the real financial information on it — and a good deal of cash hidden away.'

'Yes, but where, guv?' asked Bugsy. 'We turned that place inside out and the most suspicious items we found were a few old monks' habits in one of the sheds — probably left over from when the place was a convent. I'd like to have another look round when they don't know we're coming.'

'Me too,' agreed Jack, 'but we'll never get another warrant — not without new evidence. Chief Superintendent Garwood had to call in a favour to get the first one. If we go in without a warrant, anything we find will be inadmissible.'

It went quiet while the team wondered what they could do next.

'Sir, what about Mae — I mean, Miss Hargreaves?' asked Aled. 'She could have another poke about without raising any suspicions. If she finds anything, then we could make it official and we'd know where to look. You said she offered to help if she could.'

'That's right,' said Jack. 'She intimated that something evil was going on and she'd been fond of Charlie. She wouldn't believe he died from taking drugs. I don't want to put her in a position of danger, though.'

'Come on, guv,' replied Bugsy. 'I doubt if there's anything more dangerous than being the target of a potential hit by the mob.'

CHAPTER TWENTY

Since the police raid followed by Len and Trottie's decamp to Switzerland, things had quietened down at the Foundation. Gideon still mooched about at night, Howard and Harriet continued to garden and provide nourishing meals from the produce and Georgia stayed mainly in her room now that Charlie was no longer there. She was still hoping the police would uncover the truth behind her brother's suicide. Occasionally, she would join Rushil's yoga class — it afforded her a degree of calm. The rest of the commune continued to sing songs, plant twigs for the fairies, avoid remand and write their memoirs, blissfully unaware of the volcano of turbulence about to erupt.

Mae had been only too pleased to agree to 'have a snoop about', as Bugsy had put it. She went more or less where she pleased for Goliath's walks. The door to the Lodge was always locked when unoccupied and the blinds were down. On the one occasion that Mae had attempted to go in when the three cult leaders had been inside, Lilith had shooed her out and made it very clear that it was off limits to members at all times. Could she not read the 'No Entry' signs? The safe had been open and Mae had caught a brief glimpse of a great deal of money, probably tens of thousands, alongside packs of Lilith's playing cards and an expensive-looking camcorder. She would report all this to Inspector Dawes when she phoned him.

What Mae could not have foreseen was Lilith's innate sense of self-preservation and her antennae for danger, both of which were on constant alert. She knew Mae had probably seen more than was good for business and was wondering how best to silence her, if it became necessary. As it happened, the problem was solved for her the night that Mae decided to explore the chapel.

Goliath was sleeping quietly out of sight, between the pews. The reason for Mae's interest had nothing to do with religion. She had been puzzled by the altar. Most of the time it was bare, without even an altar cloth, which she found odd. But when the police had raided, it had been decorated with all the typical furniture that was usually present on an altar — a heavily embroidered cloth, an elaborate gold crucifix and several candlesticks. Why would the Foundation have hastily dressed it up for a visit by the police? There had also been a decorative antependium that she hadn't seen since. She approached the chancel steps, which had been of particular interest to the forensic officers. While she was on her knees, examining the stone, she heard a voice behind her.

'Verity Hargreaves? I've got a present for you — from my brother, Ronnie. You didn't think you could help the filth bang him up for twenty years and get away with it, did you?'

Mae's blood ran cold. She stood up — slowly. 'I don't know what you mean. My name's Mae. Who are you?'

'You know exactly what I mean. Couldn't mind your own business, could you? Well, I'm doing you a favour, love. You won't have to spend the rest of your life looking over your shoulder.'

As she turned around, Mae saw the vicious-looking knife in his hand. She played for time. 'How did you find me?'

He laughed. 'Witness protection's a joke. Gangs have contacts everywhere, the bloke who sold you the camper van's one of us. Easy enough for a bent copper to trace. We were just waiting for Ronnie to give the word, then . . .' He made a slashing motion across his throat.

Mae was thinking fast — wondering if she could outrun him to the door. Probably not. He was a skinny, weasel-ly-looking specimen, probably fast on his feet due to years of running from the law. 'You surely don't intend to kill me in a chapel? People come in and out all the time.'

'No, they don't. I've been watching. Nobody comes in here. It never gets used. Not exactly a God-fearing bunch, are they?' He laughed, nastily. 'They won't find your body for weeks — not until someone notices the smell and the flies. Say your prayers, love.'

He raised the knife and lunged at her. She screamed, doubting that anyone would hear — but Goliath did. Snarling and baring his teeth, he sprang out of nowhere and launched his powerful body at Mae's attacker. Taken completely by surprise, the man slashed at the dog. Goliath yelped. Despite an ugly gash, he bravely continued to defend his beloved mistress. The thug slashed at Goliath again, this time putting him down. Suddenly, there were footsteps outside on the gravel path leading to the chapel. A voice shouted, 'Hello, who's in there?'

Panicking, the man made a random lunge at Mae, slicing deep into her stomach, then ran into the vestry and out through the back door.

Unable to sleep or even settle properly, Gideon had been on one of his disturbed rambles, which had taken him past the chapel. He had heard Mae scream and Goliath yelp, then he'd called out and sprinted inside. Mae and Goliath were lying on the stone floor, their blood mingling in a rapidly increasing pool. He acted quickly. Tearing off his jacket, he rolled it up and used it to press down hard on Mae's wound. With his free hand, he pulled out his phone — grateful that he had refused to hand it over when he joined — and punched in the emergency number with his thumb.

Goliath raised his head slightly and whimpered. His tail gave a couple of feeble wags. Gideon looked at the two cruel slashes in his side. 'Hold on, boy. Hold on. I'll get help for you, too.' In the distance, he heard a car roar away down the long drive. The assailant was getting away. Too late to try to get a registration number. Lives were more important.

Minutes later, the ambulance arrived, lights flashing and sirens blaring. The paramedics ran in with their equipment and took over. Gideon used his phone to call an old friend — a vet. Mae was weak from loss of blood but still conscious. 'My dog. Please help Gollie.' She tried to reach out to him.

'It's all right, love. Take it easy.' The ambulance driver tried to calm her. 'The bloke who stopped you from bleeding out has phoned for a vet. Top man.' He turned to speak to Gideon but he'd slipped back out and disappeared into the trees.

* * *

The investigation team was mortified when the news of Mae's assault reached them, particularly Aled.

'She will be all right, won't she, sir? I'm to blame. It was my stupid, irresponsible idea to ask her to look around in the first place.'

Bugsy patted his shoulder. 'Take it easy, son. We were all in agreement and we weren't to know the mob would catch up with her while she was alone in the chapel.'

'Three cheers for Gideon,' said Gemma, without feeling much cheer. 'The hospital said she'd be dead if he hadn't stopped the bleeding. And he got a vet to Goliath a lot faster than we could have. How could that thug just walk into a chapel and attack her like that? What sort of society are we living in?'

'One that needs a robust police service,' replied Jack. Then, more gently, 'Never let your chin drop, Gemma.' He called out to Clive. 'Did we get any fingerprints from the knife?'

'No, sir. He was wearing gloves. But it was Ronnie Read's brother, all right. The clumsy sod managed to cut himself in panic when Goliath attacked, so we could match his DNA from his blood. City police have picked him up. He's been charged with attempted murder — no bail, obviously.'

'Dangerous mob but not very smart,' said Bugsy. 'That'll be both brothers banged up now.'

Jack had the serious expression on his face that indicated he was thinking hard and had hit a snag. 'Yes, but Ronnie's still running things from inside Belmarsh. He'll be even more determined to get Mae now that his brother's been arrested, if only to show the rest of the underworld that he still has power. I think Miss Hargreaves will be better off dead.'

It went very quiet. Everyone questioned what they'd heard.

'Sir?'

'Guv?'

'Jack?'

Jack explained. 'If the mob think Ronnie Read's brother was successful and Mae has died from her wounds, she won't be in danger any longer, will she?'

'I see where you're going with this, guv,' said Bugsy. 'But how will we persuade them? He didn't stick around long enough to check how badly she was injured.'

'We put an obituary notice in the *Times*. Something along the lines of "*Miss Verity Hargreaves, once principal flute with the Royal Philharmonic Orchestra, has died after a short illness. A talented lady, she will be sorely missed by her fellow musicians*," et cetera. The mob will soon pick up on it. Of course, we won't be able to charge Ronnie's brother with murder, not without a body, but attempted murder carries a long sentence, especially if you have form. What d'you think?'

'Brilliant!' exclaimed Gemma. 'She can go on living her life as Mae with Goliath looking after her. He's going to be all right, incidentally. I checked with the vet who treated him. He's all stitched together and bandaged up and feeling sorry for himself, but he'll cheer up once he can be with Mae again. Brave dog.'

'I wonder how they found her,' mused Aled. 'I mean, the Foundation of the Free Spirit isn't the first place you'd look, is it?'

'Good point, young Taffy. You know what I always say—'

'Follow the money,' they chorused.

'Correct! Unpalatable though it is, I think we have to accept that there are people out there who'll do anything for money — even some coppers.'

Jack was firm. 'For this to work, nobody — but nobody — outside this room must know that the real Verity Hargreaves isn't dead. You can rarely be completely sure who to trust — but I trust you lot. Is that understood?'

'Yes, sir.' They were convinced.

'What about Gideon, sir? He knows she's still alive. He saved her,' observed DC Mitchell.

'Yes, but he doesn't know her real identity, Mitch. To him, she's just Barmy Mae who plays the flute and wears flowers in her hat. He's the kind of bloke who performs near miracles, thinks nothing of it and moves quietly on.'

* * *

Lilith was pleased when she heard that Mae had been attacked by a knife-wielding intruder during the night. Served her right for snooping. She wouldn't be doing it again any time soon. Rumours were that she'd been taken to hospital, close to death, and her ghastly dog had actually been killed. The police had towed her camper van away, and as far as Lilith was concerned, that was the end of Mae. However, there had been too many unfortunate incidents recently and she no longer felt it was safe to continue in Kings Richington. Time to move on. A different location and a different cult name. But not until after one last Black Mass. There were some very wealthy individuals currently attending and Lilith intended to get one more large pay-off from them before she left.

Obviously, Solomon and Urbain would be coming with her. As for the rest of the pathetic cult members, they were only ever there to make up the numbers and give it some credence. She neither knew nor cared what would happen to them. Some of the more vulnerable ones may well take the same way out as the daft Delacour boy.

Solomon had been delighted when Perry had hanged himself, declaring it was a sacrifice to Astaroth. He maintained that his supplications would carry even more kudos with the Grand Duke of Hell now that he had been instrumental in the death of a young convert. Then, when that old priest Father Bartholomew had dropped dead performing an exorcism, Solomon had been so happy, he thought he'd died and gone to heaven. Lilith smiled to herself — or in Solomon's case, hell.

She wasn't sure what to do about Solomon. Urban was right, he was becoming more deranged every day. He'd always been peculiar, even as a child. She recalled their parents' horror when, at the age of ten, he'd built an altar in the back garden and sacrificed the family dog. They'd stopped short of having him analysed, but as soon as he was old enough, they'd had bundled him off to the seminary. The idea was to get his mind 'straightened out'. They little suspected that he would use his M. Div. for the purposes of devil worship and had therefore been delighted when he was ordained. What they hadn't realized was that he believed being a priest would give him more power over the black arts, which had always been his ultimate ambition. They had been spared the ignominy of seeing him unfrocked — by that time, they had both passed away.

Lilith decided that if it became unavoidable, she might have to have her brother committed before he went totally insane and ruined her whole enterprise. It would be a pity. His performances at the Black Mass had pulled in a great deal of money over the years and he'd be difficult to replace. She never ceased to be amazed at the kind of people — ostensibly respectable and certainly well heeled — who were addicted to depraved behaviour and were willing to pay large sums to become a 'disciple'. She supposed a psychologist would say that it was *because* they lived repressed lives that the concept of forbidden and, most importantly, anonymous filth appealed to them.

There were always casualties in her line of business. Sir Bixby Carrington's drinking, gambling and womanizing meant he had been a lost cause, even before she had pushed him in the lake. Amelia 'Up-Herself' Hughes-Jones was a silly, self-important cow who deserved everything she got. Charlie was a nice enough young man but couldn't keep his nose out of things that didn't concern him. She was a bit — but only a bit — sorry about him, but she couldn't allow him to hand over what he'd found on her laptop to the editor of the *Echo*, could she? She'd been telling half the truth when she told that fat sergeant there was no CCTV in the commune. There was a camera in the Lodge, obviously, because it was vital that she saw anything that went on there, and that included any activity by Solomon and Urbain. There was another camera concealed in the cloister building, where her poker sessions were held. This was how she was able to see the other players' cards, transmitted to a hidden screen under her side of the table. She had won large sums of money by cheating.

Once she'd discovered that Charlie and that airhead Georgia had broken into the Lodge, she knew that Charlie had copied files from her laptop. She also saw that he *hadn't* copied them onto the stick that Georgia had given him — only pretended to. She had searched Charlie's room thoroughly but hadn't been able to find the blasted stick. It was when he was in the refectory, obviously excited about reporting what he knew to the *Echo*'s editor, that she'd decided to drug his coffee. It hadn't worked out exactly as she'd planned. Instead of crashing outside the convent grounds, on the main road, for some reason he had ridden his bike in the opposite direction, towards the outbuildings. She guessed that's where he'd hidden the stick and he'd gone to fetch it. After he was dead, she'd searched there, too, but still hadn't found it. When days had elapsed and the *Echo* hadn't revealed what was on it nor had the police come to arrest her, she'd relaxed. That was the end of meddling Charlie.

Yes, she decided. One more Black Mass and a few more blackmail payments to collect and she would move on. She thought Somerset might be a good place. Crossed ley lines, Avalon, Glastonbury Tor, paganism and a submerged village — plenty of mystical stuff there.

CHAPTER TWENTY-ONE

Bugsy unboxed an individual fruit pie and took a huge bite. Jack knew that when his sergeant felt in need of emergency carbs, his brain had gone into overdrive. The result was always worth the wait.

'Guv, I've been thinking.' For Bugsy, this was a physical process as well as a mental one — the sharing of his thoughts was frequently accompanied by a spray of crumbs. He paused to dislodge a rogue raspberry pip from a premolar cavity. 'That Lilith woman may be evil but she isn't stupid. She knows we're getting close to whatever it is she's up to.'

'Do you think if we put more pressure on, she'll make a mistake?'

'No, I think she'll pack up and move on. New location — new victims. Clive reckoned the Foundation is a phoenix set-up, and the Honourable Georgia is convinced it's the same cult that was responsible for her brother's death operating under a different name. We have to nick Lilith and her two oppos before she vanishes and we lose her for good.'

'I agree — but the CPS won't look at it unless we can get positive and irrefutable evidence of a crime.'

'Sir, why do you suppose the mayor and the council were in favour of an exorcism?' asked Aled. 'It doesn't seem a typical reaction to what was mainly mass hysteria stirred up by the *Echo*. Nobody seriously believed the alleged sightings of wild beasts and demons in Richington Forest.'

'It seems enough of them did, to have put pressure on the councillors,' said Jack. 'What I do find hard to understand is Councillor Mrs Hughes-Jones's involvement. She was a prominent figure in local government and a staunch supporter of many charities, including the everlasting church roof fund, which most people gave up on long ago. Her colleagues said she didn't suffer fools. But according to her husband, she'd had something on her mind recently. She'd been distant and secretive. That doesn't sound in keeping with her reputation.'

'Do you think it might be a good idea to give her husband another tug?' asked Bugsy. 'The chief super interviewed him just after she died. He'd have been sympathetic but he might not have asked the right questions.'

'Mr Hughes-Jones has had time to think about it since then,' agreed Gemma. 'He might have more information to give us.'

'It's worth a try,' said Jack. 'We don't have much else.'

* * *

Paul Hughes-Jones looked ill. It was Bugsy's opinion that the 'poor sod' hadn't eaten or slept properly since his wife died. When he opened the door to the two detectives, it was almost as if he was pleased to see them.

'Please come in, officers. I've been wanting to speak to the police but I kept putting it off. Even now, I'm not sure it's the right thing to do.'

'If you have any information that will assist with our enquiries into your wife's death, sir, then it's definitely the right thing,' Jack reassured him, wondering what new horror was coming. It had been terrible enough finding the woman's body in that state. It was some comfort that she'd died from a fractured skull, but all the same . . .

'Would you like some tea?' Paul asked. 'I believe Amelia has some biscuits somewhere—' He broke off. Bugsy reckoned it would be some time yet before he stopped talking about her as if she was still alive, poor devil.

'No thank you, sir,' said Jack. 'We're fine. What is it you have to tell us?'

'It's something I want to show you, really. Would you come upstairs, please?'

He took them into the spare room and unlocked a big oak wardrobe. 'Before my wife passed, I rarely went into this room, Inspector. It's her domain. She keeps — used to keep — her council documents and charity papers here. This wardrobe, she said, was where she hung smart clothes that she wore to meetings. Suits and blouses, that kind of thing. Last week, I finally braced myself and decided I needed to give them to the charity shops she supported. The papers clearly belonged to the council and needed to be returned. Imagine my shock when I opened the wardrobe and found — *this*.' He pulled open the doors. Hanging inside was a black hooded robe, similar to those worn by monks. Around the collar was a pentacle on a chain — an inverted five-point star, inside a circle.

'What does it mean, Inspector?' Paul was mystified. 'I've never seen Amelia wearing anything like this. And look what else I found.' There were several large stones bearing runes and hieroglyphics. He opened a briefcase thinking it would contain reports of council meetings and the like. Instead, it contained a half-empty bottle of brandy and a packet of pills. 'I don't understand. Amelia never touched alcohol and she abhorred drugs of any kind. She wouldn't even take paracetamol for a headache. These things can't be hers, so why has she locked them away in the wardrobe?'

Jack and Bugsy exchanged glances. 'I really couldn't say, sir, but of course, we'll look into it — discreetly.'

'Why do you say "discreetly", Inspector? Do you think Amelia might have become involved in something inappropriate?'

That wasn't the word Bugsy would have used. Coupled with what Big Ron had told them about dried vaginal secretions, things were starting to look very sinister. But this wasn't the time to tell the poor bloke. If it was something dissolute, as Bugsy suspected, the truth would come out in the end, however discreet they were.

'It's best if we take all this off your hands, sir,' said Jack.

'Oh yes please, if you would. I really don't want to look at it.'

* * *

Back at the station, they passed the items to Forensics for testing. They found urine stains on the black hooded robe (hers), vaginal secretions (also hers) and semen (obviously not hers and with no DNA match on the database). The stones bearing the hieroglyphics had multiple fingerprints as if they'd been passed around a crowd, so offered little use for identification.

'D'you reckon we should ask her old man for a sample of his semen, Sarge?' asked Aled.

'I don't think so, son. He's been through enough and it's unlikely to be his. No, we're looking at something a bit more public than marital hanky-panky.'

DC Fox was looking at a copy of the *Echo*.

'Don't mind us, Gemma,' joshed Aled. 'We're just trying to crack a case, here.'

She ignored him. 'Where did we get this paper? It's an old copy.'

Jack looked. 'It was in with Mrs Hughes-Jones's stuff. It must have been hers. Why? Don't tell me you've found something interesting in it?'

'That'll be a first,' muttered Bugsy.

'I might have, sir. Look at this.' She passed it over.

Jack peered at it. 'It's the advert for Rushil's yoga class. My wife went with Mrs Garwood. They were doing a bit of unauthorized sleuthing until Goliath spotted them. Urban rescued them, apparently. Corrie described him as "dressed like a pox-doctor's clerk", but that expression wouldn't mean much to you kids. I reckon he—'

'No, sir, not the "upcoming events" column,' Gemma interrupted. 'Look at the "personal" column underneath.'

'The one that's ringed in red biro?'

'Yes, that's the one. What do you think that's about?'

'*You, the chosen ones, are summoned to join us in fellowship as we perform the ancient rituals. Knowledge is the greatest gift. Free yourself from ignorant enslavement,*' Jack read. 'Oh, hang on, there's more.' He read the much smaller print below. '*Entry fees and refreshments as usual. Dress code is mandatory.*'

Bugsy was looking over Jack's shoulder. 'It doesn't sound like a pensioners' tea dance in the community hall, does it? What do those letters and numbers mean at the end?'

'They're coordinates to indicate a location.' Clive was writing them down. 'And that last bit is the date, in Latin numerals.'

'So it's the time and place of a shindig,' said Bugsy.

'Not any old shindig, Sergeant,' said Jack. 'Unless I'm very wide of the mark, this is a secret gathering that led to the deaths of at least two people — possibly three.' He walked to the front and stood by the whiteboard. 'OK, troops. What have we got connecting all this supernatural nonsense?'

'Starting with the obvious, black robes with hoods have been mentioned by several witnesses,' said Aled.

'A drinking buddy of the *Echo*'s editor has come forward, claiming to have seen shadowy figures in hooded robes, making for the convent gates,' said Sergeant Parsloe. 'He also mentioned having observed "obscene goings-on" but wouldn't be more specific. He said he couldn't even bring himself to write it down.'

'Thanks, Norman. I dare say it was his chat with the editor that prompted him to put Charlie Updike in there to dig up some dirt. Anything else?'

'Other members of the public — what we front-desk jockeys describe as the "alcoholically challenged" or, if you want the technical term, "pissheads" — have mentioned seeing vampires in capes with black hoods. This was when they were taking a shortcut from the pub through Richington Forest.'

'When we interviewed Gideon, he said—' Bugsy pulled out his notebook and read — '"*I've seen what look like monks in black hooded robes. Usually three of them. They creep silently through the gates and make their way up to the convent.*"'

'An outside source — that's Mrs Dawes — reported seeing a pile of black sacks in one of the convent's outhouses,' said Jack. 'I thought it a bit odd at the time, farm sacks usually being made from brown hessian, but if Mrs Dawes says they were black, that's what they were.'

'And you reckon they might have been black robes?' said Bugsy.

'It's starting to look like it. And now we have one that we think belonged to Councillor Mrs Hughes-Jones.'

'With some suspicious stains on it,' added Gemma.

Jack sighed heavily. 'It's all pointing towards something that I've been trying to ignore until now, because it's too outrageous and too incredible to even contemplate.'

'The leaders of that cult are practising devil worship,' Bugsy finished for him.

'Not just them, Sergeant. They have somehow inveigled . . . charmed . . . deceived — whatever you want to call it — a number of upright citizens to join in. And before you say, "Follow the money," I have no doubt Lilith is making a fortune from it.'

'Not just from the "ancient ritual", which is probably just a fancy name for an orgy. I bet she films them and demands money to keep quiet,' said Mitch. 'It'd be a nice little earner. You wouldn't want your boss to see you having it away in the woods with his wife, would you?'

'I bet the poker school brings in a packet, too,' mused Gemma.

They all stared at her. 'What poker school is that?' asked Bugsy.

'Oh, didn't I mention it? When you were questioning Lilith in the Lodge, I put my head around the door to tell you about the blood that Forensics had found on the chancel steps.'

'Yep, and that was when you saw the Rolex on Urbain's wrist,' confirmed Bugsy.

Gemma nodded. 'I also saw Lilith put her foot over a poker scorecard then kick it under the table.'

'Probably dropped it when they were rushing to hide all the incriminating evidence,' said Jack.

'But where the hell did they put it all?' asked Bugsy. 'We went over that place from top to bottom.'

'I reckon that's how she got Sir Bixby's watch. He was a gambler and wouldn't have been able to resist a poker school. She'll have taken his Rolex when he ran out of cash.'

'What a piece of work,' said Bugsy. 'Preying on people's weaknesses and taking their money.'

'I think we're all agreed that the two deaths are unlikely to have been accidents, as she tried to make us believe,' said Jack. 'We have to find enough evidence to charge her and then we have to make it stick.'

CHAPTER TWENTY-TWO

'Now that we have not only murder but demanding money with menaces and a few other crimes on the charge sheet, I think we need to get up to speed with what exactly is illegal with regard to devil worship,' said Jack.

'Can't say I've come up against it before,' said Bugsy, who reckoned there was nothing in PACE that covered summoning up and arresting Satan.

'Surely, we won't need to if we can get a charge of murder, sir?' said Aled.

'No, maybe not, but demons of one sort or another underpin all the evil that's happened here. I think we should have another word with Professor MacDuff. We wrote him off as a barmy old codger last time, but you can't deny he knows his subject.'

* * *

The professor was delighted to be asked to give a talk to the team. He even brought some complimentary copies of his latest book: *The Occult and the Criminal Justice System*. Unlike many other books of the genre, there were no evocative illustrations of horned, fork-tailed devils on the cover.

It presented simply as a textbook on a serious subject, so it didn't sell many copies. MacDuff sipped the coffee offered to him and began his lecture.

'To set the scene, we must first understand that demons may be human or non-human, separable souls or discarnate spirits which have never inhabited a body. And it's necessary to distinguish clearly between a demon and the devil.'

'Aren't they the same thing?' asked someone.

'By no means. It requires a much higher development of the moral compass to give rise to the concept of a devil. "Demon", however, can be applied to beings whose harmfulness is not gratuitous but incidental to their own satisfactions.'

'And is that what we're dealing with here?' asked Jack.

The professor nodded. 'The problems involved with the modern rise of occult practices are only facets of a bigger issue confronting today's law enforcement officers. Alongside the secret practices of Satanic worship, there are the deeper problems of drugs and deviant sexual behaviour that invariably go with it.'

'Too bloody right,' whispered Bugsy.

'A police officer like yourself, Inspector Dawes, attempts to analyse these types of crime using his normal pattern of criminal investigation. This is wrong. You see, in the case of Satanic practices involving perverted sexual behaviour, you forget the offence was committed by an abnormal person — one who is influenced by many strange and complex motivations. Your investigation must therefore focus on the principles of abnormality. They are often vicious and revolting, and they create fear in the community. This is what you are dealing with here, and these situations make for sensational newspaper headlines, as we have seen in the *Echo*. I fear, Inspector, that you must brace yourself for things to become considerably worse.'

There were groans around the room. Jack doubted whether things could get much worse. 'With your in-depth knowledge of this subject, how do you suggest we proceed?' he asked.

'With great care. Occult crimes are notoriously difficult to prove. In many instances the victim is dead or confused through shock and fear. It's vital that you conduct a thorough investigation with special emphasis on the location and anything strange or unusual left at the crime scene.'

'Would that include the pentacle chalked on the tomb, Professor?' asked Gemma.

'Aye, indeed it would, lassie. In the hands of the summoner, these occult symbols are very powerful. They indicate to me that someone in this vicinity is conducting a Black Mass for criminal purposes. In order to catch, charge and prosecute this person and his acolytes, it is my opinion that you — that is, the police — must infiltrate the proceedings and catch them red-handed.'

'Or red-hoofed,' quipped Bugsy.

Professor MacDuff smiled at him. 'I get the impression, Sergeant, that you are not convinced by anything I've said.'

Bugsy shrugged. 'No offence, Prof, but does an educated man like yourself really believe all that demonic stuff?'

'We may not have caught any Satanists yet, Sergeant, but remember the wise words of the French poet, Charles Baudelaire: "*The finest trick of the devil is to persuade you that he does not exist.*"' He turned to Jack. 'Inspector, when you make your move, as I know you must, rest assured I shall be using all my powers to help you — even though you may not be aware of it at the time. You're on a dangerous crusade and you should not attempt to defeat an unknown enemy alone.'

* * *

Chez Carlene was pleasantly buzzing. At four o'clock, the bistro provided light snacks, afternoon tea, a glass of Pernod — whatever customers fancied. Corrie and Cynthia were having tea and French fancies and what Cynthia called a 'council of war' to a background of melodic French accordion music. Carlene came to join them having handed over service to Antoine.

'Right, Mrs D, Mrs Garwood. What are we doing about this demon malarkey that's going on in Richington Forest?' She produced the latest copy of the *Echo* and pointed out the new message in the personal column. 'If that isn't an invitation to something dodgy, then I'm Kylie Minogue.'

'How did you spot that?' asked Cynthia, who had no knowledge of it. As far as she knew, neither had George.

Corrie wondered if Jack and the team had seen this. He hadn't spoken to her about it, but then he wouldn't. It was another of his 'need-to-know' subjects and he wouldn't have considered she needed to know about anything potentially dangerous.

Carlene grinned. 'Antoine worked it out. Well, I sussed out the ancient rituals lark but Antoine did the sums about the time and place.'

'What d'you think's going to happen, Carlene?' Cynthia was fascinated.

'S'obvious, innit? A lot of people what ought to know better get together for some singing and dancing, a bit of gratuitous nooky, a lot of booze and some drugs. Not much different to a music festival, really.'

Corrie was impressed with the way Carlene could always take a big problem and cut it into manageable chunks. Eating an elephant sprang to mind.

'Mind you,' she continued, 'it's gone too far now. Whoever's responsible is killing people.'

Cynthia nodded. 'Bixby and Amelia were our friends. It's terrible what happened to them. Those cult people in the convent are trying to write them off as accidents.'

'Right,' agreed Carlene. 'And someone put a stop to that good-looking bloke with the red Harley. He was never an addict, like they tried to make out. You can always spot 'em. He was a reporter who got too close to the action. And poor old Father Bartholomew carked it, trying to drive out demons. He was a nice old bloke. I used to take him the odd meal.'

'How do you know all that?' asked Corrie.

'You hear a lot of stuff when you work in the takeaway business, Mrs D, especially Corrie's Kitchen. People chat while they're waiting.'

Corrie guessed that was true. She worked mainly at the high end of Coriander's Cuisine and didn't hear much gossip.

'The question is — what are we going to do about it?' asked Cynthia.

Corrie shook her head. 'Jack and the team have tried really hard but haven't come up with anything substantial to support an arrest, let alone a charge. I'm not sure there's anything we can do.'

Cynthia helped herself to the last chocolate fancy. 'I bet Carlene has a plan. What d'you reckon, Carlene?'

Carlene leaned forward and kept her voice down. 'We know where this bash is happening and we know what time. We get ourselves three black hooded robes and we join in. Be rude not to, wouldn't it?'

'How do you know they wear hooded robes?' whispered Cynthia.

'People say they've seen them, creeping through the trees,' Carlene whispered back.

'I don't think Jack would approve of that,' cautioned Corrie. 'You know what he was like the last time we "interfered".'

'This isn't interfering, Mrs D. We're just going to work undercover and finger the bad guys so Inspector Jack can nail 'em.'

'Sounds good to me.' Cynthia licked chocolate off her fingers. 'If George chews any more indigestion tablets, he'll turn into a block of chalk, like Lot's wife.'

'I think that was salt, Cynthia, but I take your point. I'm still not sure, though.'

Cynthia clocked Corrie's doubtful expression. 'Come on, Corrie. We're detectives' wives. When the going gets tough, we don't sit back and knit — we put on our big girls' pants and get stuck in.'

'OK then, we'll give it a go. But if it starts to turn nasty, we get straight out of there and phone Jack for backup.'

'Fair enough,' said Cynthia, wiping cream off her chin. 'The Three Cs are back in business! Hurrah!'

Corrie and Carlene rolled their eyes and pulled long-suffering faces.

CHAPTER TWENTY-THREE

The phone rang in the incident room. Gemma answered it. The rest of the team were drawing diagrams on the white-board, working out how many officers they were going to need on the night of the raid on the Black Mass. It hadn't been rocket science for them to find it advertised in a current copy of the *Echo*, just as the Three Cs had.

'Sir, it's the desk sergeant downstairs. He says there's a scruffy bloke in flared jeans and sunglasses wanting to speak to you. It sounds like Gideon, sir.'

'Tell the sergeant to send him up. He isn't a time-waster — far from it. If he wants to tell us something, it'll be important.'

Gideon was shown in by a constable. Jack indicated a chair. 'What can we do for you, sir?' The man looked drawn, with dark circles under his eyes.

'It's a message from Mae, Inspector. I'm not sure how important it is, but she was emphatic that I should pass it on.'

'How is the lady?' Aled still felt uncomfortable that she'd been attacked after he'd suggested she should have a snoop around the convent.

'She's doing OK. They were taking her down to theatre to have the damage to her abdomen repaired. As she was wheeled past on a trolley, she reached out a hand to me. She was well sedated and I could only just hear her. This is going to sound obscure, Inspector. She said I was to ask you, "Why was there a padlock on the altar?"'

'Was that all?' asked Bugsy.

'That — and would I look after Goliath until she was well again. Naturally, I said I would. Well, that's it, Inspector. Make of it what you will. I won't take up any more of your time. It's just that I promised Mae I'd tell you.' He stood up, nodded to the team and Gemma showed him out.

'Mae was in the chapel when she was attacked,' recalled Aled. 'She must have noticed a padlock but she's only just remembered it.'

'I'm not surprised, poor woman,' said Mitch. 'Getting a knife in your guts would tend to put anything else out of your mind.'

'Why the hell would anyone put a padlock on an altar?' wondered Bugsy.

'Maybe you store the valuable religious stuff inside it,' offered Aled.

'I don't think so,' said Gemma. 'Things like the chalice, altar cloths and holy oils are kept inside the sacristy. I didn't think you could open an altar like a cupboard.'

Jack had said nothing so far. 'Maybe you can open this one. Maybe it's specially designed for that purpose. Aled, you have the report of the search on your computer. Tell me, did we search the altar?'

Aled tapped away. 'From what I can see, sir, we searched the chapel with particular attention to the chancel steps where Forensics found the blood. Nobody touched the altar because it had a crucifix and candles and other ornaments on it. I don't suppose anyone wanted to disturb those.'

'And that's exactly what the buggers were banking on! That we'd be too respectful to rummage around on an altar. When my wife and Mrs Garwood were in there, they said the altar was bare. Even had a layer of dust on it. They'll have put all the religious furniture on it when they saw us coming up the drive.'

'So do you reckon all the incriminating evidence was locked inside the altar, guv?' asked Bugsy.

'Yes, I do, and it has been all along. They were laughing at us, searching outhouses and cloisters, knowing we wouldn't find anything that would put them away.'

Bugsy rubbed his hands together. 'Right! Let's get in there. I reckon we'll find evidence of all the rackets they've got going on — blackmail, illegal gambling, drug dealing—'

Jack stopped him. 'But not evidence of murder. That's what we really want. Something to put them behind bars for life. I doubt whether that Lilith character would be stupid enough to incriminate herself in murder, even though I'm sure she was responsible for all three. No, Sergeant, I'm sure the best way to handle this is the way Professor MacDuff recommended. Tomorrow is the night of the demons. We wait, lay an ambush and jump them.'

'And all the other idiots daft enough to be involved,' agreed Mitch.

Jack nodded. 'All leave is cancelled. I want everyone on duty.'

'OK, guv, we'll do it your way.' Bugsy had been looking forward to the expressions on their faces when they knew they'd been rumbled. It would keep.

* * *

Later that evening, Aled and Gemma were having a relaxing drink in the Richington Arms. Things were hotting up at last, and they were both on edge. Aled returned to their table with two half-pints of lager and a couple of packets of crisps.

'Gemma, I'm going to need your help with something.'

She wondered what was coming. If he wanted a shirt ironed or a button sewn on, he could whistle. 'Depends what it is.'

'It's important or I wouldn't ask.'

'OK, fire away.'

'I'm going to break into the convent and find out what's inside the altar.'

She nearly choked on her lager. 'No you're bloody well not! Are you mad?'

'No, I'm not mad, but I feel guilty about Mae nearly getting killed because I suggested she looked around. The boss said he didn't want to put her in danger and it was my fault she was hurt. She came up with a clue and I think we owe it to her to follow it up.'

'Aled, that's bollocks and you know it. And anyway, we're making the hit tomorrow night. We'll get everything we need then.'

'What if we don't? What if all we can get them for is a bit of fannying about in the woods playing at devil worship? We don't arrest people for Halloween parties, do we? And that's all it is, when you come right down to it.'

'You mustn't do this, Aled. For a start, it's too dangerous and for another thing, the boss'll be furious when he finds out. He'll probably suspend you.'

'Not if I come back with evidence of the murders.'

She looked him straight in the eye. 'You're not just doing this to get ahead of me in promotion to sergeant?'

'No, course not.'

'You won't find anything. Lilith will see you coming up that long drive like she did when we raided the place. She'll never let you in.'

'Which is why I'm going to climb over the wall. That's where you come in. I can't scale a twelve-foot wall on my own — I've tried. You're about five foot seven and I'm six foot. If I stand on your shoulders and you give me a boost up, I reckon I can just about do it.'

'I see — and how are you going to get back?'

'I've picked a spot where there's a tree on the other side. I can swing myself down from that. Then we do it all in reverse when I come out. What d'you say, Gem? Will you help me?'

She hesitated. 'Yes, all right. I must be crackers but I don't want to be responsible for you breaking your neck. What time do we start?'

'I thought midnight would be good. Wear something dark.'

'OK, I'll fish out my little black cocktail dress, shall I?' She rolled her eyes. 'Get me another drink — I'll have whisky this time.'

* * *

There was a full moon when Aled and Gemma reached the convent. Both dressed in black, they looked like a couple of cat burglars. Aled had marked the spot with chalk where he intended to scale the wall. It was the furthest point from the Lodge House and close to where Charlie had crashed his bike.

'Promise me you'll be careful,' urged Gemma.

'Course I will, I'm a copper, aren't I?'

'Have you got the bolt-cutters for the padlock?'

'Yep. Right, crouch down while I stand on your shoulders, then up we go.'

With a good deal of grunting and heaving, Gemma hoisted him up and he got his arms over the top of the wall. She could hear him rustling the branches of the tree on the other side as he jumped down. 'I'm in,' he called in a hoarse whisper. 'Wait for me. I won't be long. Half an hour, tops.'

Gemma looked at her watch. It was half past midnight. She still wondered why she'd agreed to this, but she couldn't have let the silly little sod do it on his own. She sat down on the grass with her back to the wall and waited.

Aled made his way to the chapel down the long track, keeping close to the buildings so he wouldn't be spotted. The heavy chapel door was ajar. This was good. He could slip inside without making any noise.

He crept down the aisle and approached the altar, which was bare, just as Mrs Dawes had reported. He pulled out the bolt-cutters and shone his torch, looking for the padlock.

There wasn't one. He leaned forward to lift the lid and a statuette of the devil came crashing down on his head. He slumped, unconscious, on the chancel steps with blood seeping from the wound.

Solomon stood looking down at what was the second body to lie bleeding on the chancel steps — but this one was still alive. His first instinct was to run to the Lodge House and tell Lilith what he'd done. Whenever he'd committed some misdemeanour as a child, he had always run to tell his big sister, but this time he hesitated. Tomorrow was the night of the demons. Everything he lived for centred around those Friday nights when he felt the power of the black sacrament coursing through his veins as he summoned Astaroth. It was far stronger than anything he'd felt as a Catholic priest. But this time — he trembled at the very thought — this time, he had a live sacrifice to offer to the Grand Duke of Hell. How much more powerful would be the invocation, how much respect it would earn him from demons and disciples alike.

If he told Lilith, she would try to stop him. This would be the last Black Mass in Kings Richington, as Lilith had said they were moving on. He had a large following here and he wanted to show them the full extent of his power. He would demonstrate how ineffective the old priest's exorcism had been against Astaroth.

He needed somewhere to keep this nosey young copper until tomorrow night. He was one of the fascists who had taken part in the police raid on the convent. Solomon had recognized him from the moment he came into the chapel, despite his attempt to disguise himself in those black clothes. He needed to think fast, before the man came round. He would keep him drugged — there was always plenty available while Urbain was around. He'd be out of sight, tied up in one of the disused sheds until the time came to offer him up on the tomb. He was so excited, he could hardly breathe. Solomon had no way of knowing that he was descending rapidly into the final stages of the insanity that had threatened to engulf him all his life.

* * *

It was four in the morning when Gemma woke up. She was stiff with cold and damp from the grass that had seeped through the seat of her trousers. She stood up and rubbed the life back into her arms and legs. Where the hell was Aled? He'd said he wouldn't be more than half an hour. Just long enough to find out what was hidden in the altar and take some photos on his phone. There was no way she could go in and find him — she'd never get over the wall on her own.

She decided he must have come out a different way and forgotten about her. She pulled out her phone and tried his mobile. He'd switched it off — probably didn't want it to ring while he was creeping about in the chapel. Well, he could have had the decency to switch it back on when he came out and let her know he was all right! That was the last time she was going to help him with one of his hare-brained ideas.

She made her way back to where she'd hidden her car and went home for a hot bath and some coffee. Early start tomorrow. Final briefing for everyone taking part in Operation Demon Killer, which was pretty much the whole station.

CHAPTER TWENTY-FOUR

Next morning, at breakfast, both Jack and Corrie were wondering how to explain that they would be out late that Friday night. Jack didn't want to tell Corrie where he would be and what he would be doing. Operation Demon Killer was top secret. He was well aware that the police had little knowledge of exactly who would be at the Black Mass. If it got out, half of them wouldn't turn up and the main protagonists would do a runner. In addition, he didn't want to worry her.

Corrie had no idea that the police were planning an ambush. For her part, she and her two accomplices were simply intending to join the crowd of devil-worshippers to find out who was behind it. She didn't dare tell Jack or he would forbid her to go.

They each had their alibis ready.

'I've volunteered to help Carlene out at the bistro tonight,' Corrie lied. 'Friday night is always busy and she's taken lots of bookings. By the time we've cleared up, I probably won't be home until gone midnight.'

'That's all right, sweetheart,' said Jack. 'Bugsy and I thought we'd have a boys' night out. We haven't been out for a meal together since he married Iris. It'll be like old times. Don't wait up for me.'

It was much the same in the Garwood household. George told Cynthia he had a Lodge meeting and would be very late. She explained that she had planned a late-night supper with the fundraising committee from the Inner Wheel Club. All was ready.

* * *

By late evening, the weather had turned. The end of the recent spell of hot, humid weather finally erupted into a violent thunderstorm with lightning and hurricane-force winds. Solomon was delighted. The flashing and crashing would be a perfect accompaniment to his deadly ritual. He had planned it down to the last detail — the sacrificial dagger with a pentacle engraved on the handle was hidden in the curly black goatskin outfit that he wore below the waist. The goat head stood ready, with the black candle between its horns. Solomon planned to catch the blood of his sacrifice in the human skull and fling it over the disciples, while summoning Astaroth to the glorious invocation in his honour.

Aled had regained consciousness of a kind, very briefly. It was dark and he couldn't move. For a few moments, he remembered the blow on the head, wondered vaguely why he was tied and gagged, then drifted back into drugged oblivion.

* * *

The atmosphere at the station was electric. All officers were in a state of high energy, anticipating a night of vigorous policing. Thunder and lightning raged outside and the wind was bringing down trees.

'Where's young Taffy?' Bugsy asked Gemma. 'I haven't seen him all day. He should be here, ready for the inspector's final briefing.'

Gemma hesitated. She didn't want to shop Aled but she was starting to worry. His mobile was still turned off. If she told the sergeant what they'd been up to the previous night, it would get them both into trouble, and she wouldn't put it past Aled to come swanning in at the last minute with some excuse about where he'd been all day. She decided to stall. 'Dunno, Sarge. Maybe he isn't well.'

'It isn't like the lad not to let anyone know.' He looked at her, suspiciously. 'You sure you don't know where he is? You're thick as thieves, you two.'

'No, Sarge. I haven't a clue.' She crossed her fingers behind her back and hoped nothing had happened to the daft Welsh plonker.

Jack strode to the front and raised a hand for quiet. 'You all know what you have to do. We don't know whether any laws will be broken tonight, but we know they have been in the past. It's our job to identify the miscreants and arrest them, even if it's only for affray or violent disorder.'

'D'you reckon they'll come quietly, sir?' asked someone at the back.

Chief Superintendent Garwood answered from the doorway. 'If they're innocent, Constable, they have nothing to fear from the police. If they're guilty of the heinous crimes that we suspect, then we take them — quietly or not.'

'Blimey,' muttered Bugsy. 'Is the old man coming with us?'

Garwood heard. 'Yes, Sergeant, the "old man" is coming with you. I want to be present when we arrest those responsible for the deaths of some good people.'

* * *

Cynthia, Corrie and Carlene were piling into Corrie's car. They'd originally decided that Cynthia should drive, but she'd had what she described as a 'couple of stiffeners' before she left home — *'Just a couple of teensy-weensy gins to brace me.'*

The trio were wearing black robes with the hoods up, hired from a fancy dress shop and originally intended for Halloween parties.

Corrie giggled. 'I don't know about going by car — we look like we should be flying in on broomsticks.'

'Not in this storm, Mrs D. We'd end up stuck in a tree.'

Carlene little realized that being stuck in a tree would be the cause of a terrifying situation later.

* * *

Solomon was hiding deep in Richington Forest, waiting for the throng to gather and the chant to begin — the cue for his dramatic entrance. It was indeed a perfect night for demons. He was ecstatic. The wind howled through the trees like a soul in torment. Several of the weaker beech trees lay creaking, felled by the battering gales and lightning strikes. This, Solomon believed, was Astaroth showing his approval for what his servant was about to do.

He had bound Aled to the tomb slab. The young officer was still gagged but the drugs were slowly wearing off. He was covered with a heavy, gold altar cloth embroidered with serpents, symbols and runes. Aled was tall but slightly built, so it had been no effort for Solomon, strong and muscular, to drag him to the clearing and hoist him onto the chest tomb. Added to which, Solomon now had the superhuman strength of a madman on a mission.

Stealthily, the followers slunk in from around the forest. As they joined the circle, they drank from the chalice of drugged sacramental wine and nibbled on wafers of blackened bread — an abomination of the Holy Communion. If they noticed the unusual outline of a figure on the tomb, they didn't approach it. The atmosphere was heavy with foreboding. Gradually, they began to shuffle, side by side, until the circle was complete. The chanting began. '*Ave Satanas* — Hail Satan.'

Beneath the altar cloth, Aled was emerging from his drugged state. He could neither move nor speak — but he could hear. He had no idea where he was or how long he'd been there. The events of the previous night slowly filtered back into his confused mind. He'd been in the chapel when someone had hit him with a heavy object. He must have been knocked unconscious. Gemma! Where was Gemma? He'd left her outside the wall. She would have raised the alarm by now. The troops would be on the way to find him and break this up.

In her usual place, out of sight with her camcorder, Lilith saw the concealed outline of a figure on the tomb and wondered what on earth Solomon was up to now. If that was a body, he must have persuaded one of his 'flock' to take part in some wacky ritual. Usually, it was a woman willing to undergo his 'initiation ceremony'. There were some really desperate women out there who'd do anything to be the centre of attention. She hoped this one was rich and would just hand over whatever she was asked for without argument, unlike the Hughes-Jones woman. This was to be her last haul before moving on and she wanted it to be a big one — enough to set them up comfortably and start a new cult in the mystic wilds of Somerset.

* * *

Jack, Bugsy and Garwood were travelling in the same car, driven by Mitch, heading up a long convoy of police cars, vans and emergency vehicles. Garwood had called up armed response teams and dog handlers. The roads were strewn with debris — branches of trees, bins that had blown over — and when they got out into the country, whole trees were down and parts of hedges had been buffeted loose. Jack had instructed no blues and twos. He didn't want any of the suspects to escape before they could be detained for questioning and arrest.

Garwood was getting impatient. 'Can't you go any faster, Mitchell? It's half past eleven. We have to catch them in the act, otherwise it's a great deal out of the overtime budget for nothing. Put your foot down, man!'

'Sorry, sir. I'm trying to avoid the rubbish being chucked about by the gale.'

Several flashes of lightning lit the sky, immediately followed by a deafening crash of thunder. The storm was right above them. There were no lights along the road due to widespread power cuts, so Mitch was relying solely on his headlights. As a result of Garwood urging him to put his foot down, he increased his speed to what he regarded as risky. And so it turned out. Around the next bend, an elderly and decaying oak had given up the fight and crashed down across the road. Unable to brake in time, Mitch smashed headlong into it. The domino effect meant at least half a dozen of the cars in the convoy concertinaed into one another.

'Oh, bloody well done, Constable! That's all we need.' Garwood was seething. 'Didn't you see that tree? God knows it's big enough.'

'Can we get around it, Mitch?' asked Jack, more calmly.

''Fraid not, sir. This is a single-track road. There's only room for one vehicle with occasional passing places.'

'Well, now what do you suggest we do? Get out and walk?' barked Garwood.

'It's too far to walk, sir,' explained Jack. 'By the time we get there, it'll all be over and we'll have lost them. I suggest we radio the other cars and tell them to back up. There's a lane to the left about a mile back that will take us to the site, albeit by a longer route.'

'All right,' grumbled Garwood. 'Well, get on with it, then.'

Gemma was travelling in the car behind with Sergeant Parsloe and two uniformed constables. When they ran into the back of the chief super's car, she was glad she hadn't been driving. Then the car behind smashed into them and she felt the whiplash streak through her neck. She was really angry with Aled. No sign of him when they left and his phone was still switched off. What was he playing at? Being a copper was more than just important to him — it was his whole life. He'd told her that it was all he'd ever wanted to do, right since he was a little boy. How chuffed he'd been when he was promoted to detective constable. The way he was behaving now, he'd be lucky to have a job at all, never mind with the MIT! At the same time, a small voice in her head was dreadfully afraid that something had happened to him. She decided that as soon as they reached the crime scene, she would have a word with Sergeant Malone. He'd know what to do.

CHAPTER TWENTY-FIVE

The chanting reached a crescendo and the circling became faster. Corrie, Cynthia and Carlene had only pretended to drink the drugged alcohol, and had joined the throng right at the back, so as not to be conspicuous, although with everyone in hooded robes, it was impossible to tell who was next to you. Carlene feared they may have become separated in the fevered whirling.

'Mrs D, is that you?' Carlene grasped the hand of the person on her right. He responded with a squeeze and shuffled closer, putting his arm around her.

'I'm here, Carlene.' Corrie's voice came from Carlene's left. 'I don't know where Cynthia has gone. I think she lost her way in the crowd.'

The noise of the chanting, coupled with the rumbles and cracks of thunder from the storm and the wind tearing through the trees meant that they had to shout to be heard. Carlene struggled free from the amorous intentions of her neighbour and grasped Corrie's hand instead.

'Never mind,' said Corrie. 'We'll find her when this is over. She'll need a lift home. What do you suppose that is, on the tomb?'

'Dunno. A dummy of some kind, I expect,' replied Carlene. 'This would be quite scary if it wasn't daft.'

The rain that had been threatening for some time erupted into a deluge. The acolytes were soaked in minutes. Far from putting them off, it seemed to whip them into an even wilder frenzy. Some of them threw open their robes to let the rain drench their naked bodies.

'Why would all these people come out here in this terrible weather?' yelled Corrie, trying to keep up with the wild gyrating. She wished she'd worn wellingtons instead of trainers.

Carlene was her normal, pragmatic self, despite the far-from-normal circumstances. 'Looking for a piss-up, a few uppers and a bit of random shagging, I guess,' she yelled back. 'Mind you, they could get that in any of the clubs in town. At least it would be dry and you could see who you were having it off with.' She pointed to a gap in the trees where a light flickered. 'Look out, Mrs D, I think it's showtime.'

A figure with a goat's head emerged from the forest, his smooth, muscular torso wet and glistening. The curly black hair that sprouted from the hind legs was matted and the cloven hooves dug deep into the mud, slowing his progress. He shouted above the raging storm: 'Stop! *In nomine dei nostri Satanas Luciferi Excelsi.* I order you to stop — in the name of our God, Satan, Lucifer of the Most High.'

The black candle between his horns was never going to stay alight in the pelting rain, so Solomon had improvised with a portable black lantern. While it wasn't quite as menacing as a candle, he felt it was sufficient to provide the ominous light he needed to illuminate the sacrifice. It was a pity, but the trick with the blazing statuette of Satan wouldn't work in this weather, either. Flames would have been the perfect climax for when he drove the dagger home. He had also ditched the contact lenses he used to make his eyes glow like hot coals in the dark. He had been worried the rain might wash them out.

On his arrival, the worshippers fell to their knees on the wet grass, some of the older ones fearing the effect on their arthritis. Most of them had abandoned their candles in favour of torches. As the goat figure passed around the circle, each devotee rose up and switched theirs on. Corrie and Carlene hadn't brought torches so used the light on their mobiles. Once he was in front of her, Corrie took the opportunity to have a good look at the man behind the make-up and other theatrical nonsense. She was sure she could recognize him if required.

At the end of this part of the ritual, Solomon ran to the tomb and whipped off the altar cloth with a flamboyant flourish. Aled could now see as well as hear what was happening. The crowd gasped then chanted, 'Astaroth — Beelzebub — Lucifer — hear us!'

From her position in the trees, Lilith wondered what this new performance of Solomon's was about. She was too far away to see who he'd persuaded to take part in it but she could tell it wasn't a woman. She doubted it would elicit much in the way of income. Her interest from a video aspect was in the final part of the mass — the orgy. She knew from the entrance requests that there were a number of important figures out there who would pay handsomely to keep their 'hobby' secret.

Sensing something out of the ordinary, the crowd became restless. The chant became a roar, which pushed Solomon to more extremes. This was wonderful! How strong would his powers of summoning be after this? He leaped up onto the end of the tomb, one hoof either side of Aled's head. With newly enhanced strength and agility, his arms outstretched in supplication, he pointed two fingers up and two down — the devil's horns.

'Within this circle, I call thee. Within this circle, I bind thee. Within this circle, I summon thee. Astaroth, I call thee forth to witness this sacrifice I make to thee.' He bent and drew out the huge sacrificial dagger, hidden in his goatskin tights. The crowd gasped. So did Aled.

* * *

Still at least a mile away, the convoy of police vehicles was meandering through flooded lanes on the outskirts of the forest. The reversing process had been slower than anticipated due to the poor visibility and the number of vehicles involved. Garwood hadn't helped, shouting on his radio at the poor unfortunate drivers who weren't reversing as fast as he wanted. In the back, Jack and Bugsy were looking at their watches anxiously.

'Bugsy, if we don't catch these bastards in the act of a crime, so we can detain them without bail, they'll leg it and we'll never find them. New location, new names and a new racket.'

'I know, guv, and we have to make it stick. You know what the CPS is like. Mention Black Mass and orgies and they'll tell us to go and do a proper job, catching real criminals, not a bunch of clowns fannying about in the woods.'

'What we mustn't forget,' said Garwood from the front seat, 'is that this "bunch of clowns" is responsible for at least three murders, never mind accessories in drug dealing, perverting the course of justice and blackmail. Once we've got them in the cells, I'm sure we'll be able to add several more crimes to the charge sheet.'

After what seemed like an eternity, the reversing convoy finally reached the diversion, leading to the forest.

Garwood shouted into his radio. 'Right, all cars, step on it!'

* * *

Solomon was squeezing every bit of melodrama out of his performance. He called upon all the demons in hell to behold his allegiance to Astaroth. The human skull stood ready to catch the blood of his sacrifice.

Corrie pulled Carlene's hood to one side and put her mouth close to her ear.

'Are you sure that's a dummy?'

'No, Mrs D,' Carlene was worried. 'I think I saw it move.'

'Me too. I don't like this.' She pulled out her phone. 'We agreed if it went tits up, we'd call the police. I'm going to call Jack.' Corrie eased herself out of the circle of spectators, who were baying like a football crowd just before a penalty kick.

When Jack's mobile rang, he saw from the number that it was Corrie. He could hear loud crowd noises in the background. 'Corrie? Where are you? I thought you were helping Carlene out at the bistro.'

Corrie cupped her hands over her phone, trying to make herself heard. 'I'm sorry to interrupt your night out with Bugsy, but we need you here.'

Jack strained his ears to hear what she was saying. 'Why, is there trouble at the bistro?'

'No, we're not at the bistro.' Corrie took a deep breath. Jack wasn't going to like this. 'We're in Richington Forest. Jack, there's some sort of Black Mass going on. There's a bloke dressed up like a goat and he's got a huge knife. He's pretending to perform a human sacrifice — but I'm not sure he's pretending.'

Jack was horrified. 'Corrie, what the hell were you thinking? Stay close to Carlene — we're on our way.' He leaned forward to speak to Garwood. 'That was my wife, sir. She's at the scene. She says things have turned nasty and one of the cult leaders is brandishing a knife.'

'Good God, man! What's your wife doing there? Have you no control over her? Mrs Garwood would never put herself at risk like that.' He spoke to DC Mitchell. 'How long before we reach the perimeter, Constable?'

'At least another ten minutes, sir.'

Garwood radioed Armed Response. 'Stand by to deploy your team as soon as location is identified. At least one suspect is brandishing a weapon.'

Bugsy was worried. 'Guv, did I hear you say Mrs Dawes and Carlene are in the thick of it? What are they doing there?'

'God only knows. They'll say they were trying to "help". Bugsy, if anything happens to them . . .'

'It won't, Jack. We'll be there soon. They're a feisty couple, they'll be fine. You'll see.' But in view of the unsolved atrocities of the past few weeks, Bugsy wasn't as confident as he sounded. He sat, clenching and unclenching his fists, willing the car to go faster so he could get stuck in.

CHAPTER TWENTY-SIX

Solomon had finished his frenzied invocation to Astaroth and Satan. He kissed the pentacle on the dagger and held it aloft in both hands, eager to plunge it into Aled's chest.

Aled was fully conscious now. *This is it*, he thought. *I'm going to die. There's no one here to help me.* He said a quick prayer for his mother and father, who had always wanted him to be a rugby player instead of a policeman. And a silent apology to Gemma, who'd tried to persuade him not to get involved but he wouldn't listen. And a tribute to Mae, the brave, flute-playing lady, whose attack he had been trying to avenge. He knew now that he shouldn't have tried to do it on his own. First rule of policing: it's teamwork. Never approach a dangerous situation without calling for backup. Now, too late, he understood why. He saw the raving lunatic standing over him and bringing the dagger down. He closed his eyes.

Carlene's eyes, however, were wide with horror. 'Bloody hell, Mrs D, tell me this is just an act. He isn't really going to stick that knife in him, is he?'

'Not if I have anything to do with it!' Corrie broke cover, shoving the drunken, drugged idiots out of the way. Carlene, hot on her heels, decided she'd grab the bloke's legs, pull him down off the tomb and jump on him. The man on her right in the circle gripped her arm to pull her back, but she shook him off. From the opposite side of the clearing, she could see Cynthia racing towards them, screaming like a banshee. Then something happened that stopped all three women in their tracks.

A hooded figure in the crowd leaped on the tomb and shoved Solomon hard in the chest. Taken completely by surprise, he lost his balance and fell heavily.

The man threw off his hood. 'Lord our God, I call upon you to intervene!' His voice was strong and commanding.

Eerily, the violent storm abated. The wind stopped howling and thunder rumbled away into the distance. He held a crucifix aloft. '*Ecce crucem Domini!* Behold, the cross of the Lord. *Fugite partes adversae!* Begone, all evil powers!'

The crowd cowered and sank to their knees. The prayer continued. 'Defend us in this night of battle. Be our safety against the wickedness and snares of the devil. We beg You to reach out Your powerful hands and raise us above all evil.'

Corrie was astonished — the more so when the man appeared to grow in stature. Not a huge amount but certainly a few inches. Her mind was playing tricks. Carlene, who had been spoiling for a fight, still had adrenalin pumping through her veins, but she saw it too.

The preacher produced a phial of holy water from beneath his robes and threw it over the cowering Solomon. 'God rebukes you! Beg His forgiveness.' Solomon screamed as if he'd been scalded, grabbed the dagger and ran off into the heart of the forest.

While the stunned crowd was trying to process this, floodlights came on all around the clearing. Garwood's voice could be heard, shouting through a megaphone. 'Stand still. Do not move. You are all under arrest!'

'Thank goodness,' breathed Corrie. 'The cavalry's here.'

'About bloody time, too!' said Cynthia. 'I was beginning to think they'd stopped off at Corrie's Kitchen for a bacon roll.'

It was mayhem after that. Some people were too shocked to move but several others tried to escape, despite being weakened by drink and drugs. Corrie recognized the chairman of a local oil company, a couple of knights of the realm and the vicar's wife. Coriander's Cuisine had catered functions for all of them at some time. Police officers were now rounding them up and shoving them into vans. The dogs were barking excitedly, eager for their handlers to send them to bring somebody down.

* * *

After several long, nerve-racking minutes, Jack found Corrie and Carlene in the melee and hugged them both with sheer relief. 'Thank goodness you're safe.'

'Course we are, Inspector Jack,' assured Carlene, squeezing the rain from her ponytail. 'Piece of cake.'

'What does it mean, please — a piece of cake?' It was the young man who had tried to pull Carlene back when she ran to help Corrie. 'I do not understand what *un morceau de gâteau* has to do with this, cherie.'

'Antoine?' squealed Carlene. 'What are you doing here?'

He put his arms around her. 'You forget — it was I who worked out the time and place from the newspaper. I knew you would go and that I could not stop you so I came, to keep you from harm.' They became entangled in a passionate embrace that Corrie thought only a Frenchman would attempt in public.

'It might not have been "*un morceau de gâteau*" without that man,' said Corrie. She pointed to the preacher who'd put a stop to the whole ghastly business in the nick of time. He came across to join them.

'Professor MacDuff?' Jack was astounded. 'I hadn't expected to see you here.'

'I promised I'd use all my powers to help you when the time came, Inspector. There was no way I was going to allow that pathetic, second-rate necromancer to harm anybody. My lady friend is untying your young police officer. I imagine he'll need some medical attention.'

They hurried to the tomb to find Bugsy and a still-hooded lady helping a wobbly Aled to stand. 'Thanks for your help, madam.'

She pushed back the hood. 'You're welcome. It's a nice change to be handling a body that's still alive.'

'Miss Catwater?' Jack and Bugsy were both surprised to recognize Big Ron's mortuary assistant.

Corrie was delighted. This must be the lady friend who shares Professor MacDuff's Caledonian Chicken that he pretends he's cooked himself.

Gemma appeared out of the posse of police officers. She sprinted across to Aled, threw her arms around him and hugged him, tightly. Then she pushed him away and slapped him, hard.

Shaken, Aled asked, 'What was that for?'

'It was for scaring the shit out of me, you dopey Welsh dick!' Then she hugged him again. 'Come on, let's get you to an ambulance.'

'Well, you guys took your time,' complained Cynthia to Jack and Bugsy. It's a good job the Three Cs had everything under control.' She spotted Garwood coming towards them from the other side of the clearing. 'Oh, blimey! There's George. I'm supposed to be at a meeting of the fundraising committee!' She pulled the hood well down over her head and ran for it.

As Garwood approached, he spotted the running figure and broke into a sprint. He yelled at Jack as he dashed past. 'There's one trying to escape! I'll get him.' He caught up just before the row of trees and rugby-tackled Cynthia to the ground, face down. 'Oh no, you don't, chummy. Didn't you hear what I said? You're under arrest.' It felt good — just like when he was a young constable, doing proper policing instead of checking overtime forms and polishing the seat with his arse most of the day. He pulled out handcuffs that he hadn't used for years but had had the forethought to bring with him, in the unlikely event that he might have to arrest someone. He snapped them on the wrists of the prisoner.

'You're coming with me.' He turned his captive over and pulled back the hood.

'Hello, George.'

'Cynthia? CYNTHIA?'

'I'll come quietly. Let's go home.' She winked. 'Can we keep the handcuffs?'

* * *

Solomon was thrashing about in the heart of the forest. Disgraced in the eyes of Astaroth, he was desperate to redeem himself. He was still smarting from the scalding holy water. On the skin of an unfrocked priest and devil-worshipper, it burned like acid. He had completely lost all sense of time and place, needing only to regain favour with the Grand Duke of Hell.

From her spot in the trees with her camcorder, Lilith had watched with mounting anger as the police had descended and destroyed the lucrative proceedings. She hadn't realized that Solomon had been stupid enough to attempt a live sacrifice — and a police officer, of all people! Solomon would have encountered him when the police had searched the Foundation, so he obviously knew he was a copper. How he believed he could get away with a murder, witnessed by upwards of fifty people, she could not imagine. It had been a close thing explaining the three murders she had already been responsible for.

There was nothing left now but to decamp quickly, before they could be arrested. No explanation, however devious and clever, would get them out of this mess. She would go back, briefly, for the money and the laptop with all the financial transactions on it. There were also incriminating details about how she had blackmailed her victims and copies of video evidence. It wouldn't do for those to fall into the wrong hands. Then she would find Solomon, load the van that she kept hidden away for a quick exit and leave. They could be miles away by morning. Urbain could take care of himself.

As it turned out, she didn't need to find Solomon — he found her. He appeared from among the bushes, wild-eyed and manic.

'There you are, Solomon. We have to leave immediately. Come with me, collect a few things and we'll go before the police catch up with us. Once they've processed all the people they've arrested, they'll make straight for the Foundation.'

Solomon glared at her as if he didn't understand.

'Come on! There's no time.' She tried to take his hand which was when she realized that he was still holding the dagger.

'It's your fault,' snarled Solomon, turning on her. 'If you hadn't called down the wrath of the non-believer — that servant of the anti-Satan — I should now have great power, the ability to bring about the destruction of those who would deny the needs and desires of a true Satanist.'

'Solomon, pull yourself together. You know this whole charade was merely to bring out the baser instincts in your "disciples" so we could make money from them. You can't really summon the devil. It was just a game like you used to play as a little boy. But now we have to go.' Lilith could hear the baying of the police dogs as they searched the forest for Solomon and, above anyone, her.

Solomon pushed her to the ground. '*Ave, Satanas.* Hear me, Astaroth! Behold the sacrifice I make. Take this woman who would deny your omnipotence. May she burn in your everlasting hell.'

He raised the dagger. Lilith realized her little brother had crossed the Rubicon into total insanity. There was no way back for him. She could see the lights of the police search team coming closer. She tried to stall until they reached her.

'Solomon, please. Don't do this. It will be all right. I'll look after you, like I always have.'

'Astaroth is my keeper.' He plunged the dagger deep into her heart.

The search team found Solomon sitting beside his sister's body, muttering entreaties to Astaroth, the bloodied dagger lying in the grass. They checked Lilith for a pulse, but she was dead and this was now a crime scene. One of the officers radioed it in. Another officer took Solomon by the elbow and helped him to his feet.

'Come along, now, sir. You need to come with us.' The officer snapped on handcuffs but Solomon offered no resistance. They took him to where the police vehicles were lined up in the road and put him in a van. He continued to have a one-way conversation with Astaroth right up until men in white coats came to take him.

CHAPTER TWENTY-SEVEN

The post-mortem on Lilith was brief and uncomplicated. Jack, Bugsy and Gemma attended. Aled had wanted to, but the doctor had said he must stay in hospital 'until the filthy cocktail of drugs that some madman had injected into him had been flushed out of his system'.

The mortuary room was cold with glaring white tiles and the sickly, antiseptic smell that always caught in Jack's throat. He did his best not to dry retch. The smell still had that effect on him, despite the number of years he'd been doing this job.

'No mystery regarding cause of death, officers,' announced Dr Hardacre. 'The deceased was stabbed through the heart with this.' She held up a specimen bag containing the dagger. 'She would have died instantly.' She regarded the weapon with a pathologist's impartial, rather than morbid, interest. 'Nasty piece of kit. Sharp as a cut-throat razor. Marigold said it was intended for a human sacrifice — your young Detective Constable Williams.'

'That's right,' said Jack. 'Thanks to Professor MacDuff, it didn't happen, but it was a close-run thing.'

'MacDuff isn't quite as mad as a box of frogs, then?' Dr Hardacre conceded. 'I'm glad. DC Williams is a good lad.

His heart's in the right place — and that place isn't here in one of my organ dishes.'

'Maybe his brain should be,' muttered Gemma. She hadn't yet forgiven him for the scare he'd given her.

* * *

Outside, Gemma remonstrated with herself. 'He really thought he'd be safe going in there alone, and the worst of it is, I helped him. If he'd been killed, it would have been my fault for not stopping him. I should have raised the alarm as soon as he went missing.' Tears welled up.

Bugsy pulled out a handkerchief stained with something red. It could have been anything edible — ketchup, fruit pie, pizza — but he was confident it wasn't blood. He offered it to her. 'Don't get upset, love. It was the wrong tree, that's all.'

She sniffed. 'You mean the one he climbed down, to get in there?'

'No — I mean the one he was barking up. It's true the evidence we wanted to find was actually locked inside the altar at the time we searched. They relied on the fact that our lads wouldn't ransack a religious item that had a crucifix, candles and all the other sacred paraphernalia on it. But by the time young Taffy broke in, the evidence was back in the safe. So even if he hadn't got his head bashed in, he wouldn't have found it.'

Jack nodded. 'Fair play to Aled for trying. OK, he wasn't following PACE guidance, but I'm the last one to point that out.'

'Ways and Means Act, guv. The doc reckons Taffy's going to be fine.'

* * *

With Lilith and Solomon out of the picture, only Urbain remained of the criminal trinity. By the time the police returned to the convent, he was long gone.

'Do you suppose he's given up, sir?' asked Aled. He was still very pale but had insisted he was well enough to return to work.

'Drug dealers never give up, Aled. They're like vultures — they just move to another tree. Bernie Bottle will find another place to ply his trade, hopefully well away from Kings Richington. Unless we can find something to prove he had a hand in the murders, he'll get away with it.'

'Are we going to question Solomon, sir?' Gemma wondered.

'No. He was assessed by the police psychiatrist and he's been sectioned. There's no way he'll ever be fit to be interviewed or stand trial.'

'There's an argument that says there's no such thing as madness — only varying degrees of sanity,' mused Bugsy. 'Solomon was right off the Richter scale. According to the report, he told the psychiatrist that Astaroth would send forty legions of demons to free him from the non-believers. Since he sacrificed his sister, he has been elevated to the rank of twenty-ninth spirit — a crowned Prince of Chaos.'

'Is it true he was once a priest?' asked Aled.

'Yep,' said Bugsy. 'He was unfrocked for joining the opposition. A bit like an MP crossing the floor of the House.'

'What will happen to the people left in the convent?' asked Gemma. 'Some of them won't be able to cope on their own. The last time I was there, two of them were planting mushrooms for the elves to sit on.'

'I think the council is getting involved with regard to a change of use,' said Jack. 'Before that happens, though, we need to do another thorough trawl without any interference. The chief super wants all the loose ends tied up.'

* * *

Back at the station, Sergeant Parsloe reported that a couple had come to the front desk and handed in a padded envelope that they said was for Inspector Dawes's eyes only.

Jack opened it. 'Unless I'm much mistaken, this is Charlie Updike's phone and memory stick. What did the couple look like, Norman?'

Parsloe scratched his head. 'She was wearing dungarees and he was in an old jacket like the one I wear for gardening. They didn't leave their names — said there was a note inside that would explain everything.'

Jack pulled it out.

Dear Inspector Dawes,

We found these items in one of the sheds Charlie used. We didn't hand them over after he died because we felt they were private to him and should be given to his next of kin. We have since found out that he was brought up in a children's home and didn't have a next of kin, so we are entrusting them to your care, knowing you will do what's right. Thank you.

Yours sincerely,
Howard and Harriet.

P.S. Charlie did NOT take drugs. Please find out what really happened to him.

Jack handed the phone and stick over to Clive and his team of techies. 'Clive, I need you to apply your massive geek brain to anything you can find on these. We believe Charlie Updike downloaded stuff from Lilith's computer.'

Clive plugged in the stick and tapped some keys. 'Blimey, sir, the woman was encryption-mad. It isn't impossible to decipher but it's going to take some time.'

'Fair enough, we'll leave you to it.' He gestured to the rest of the team. 'Come on, troops, we're going back to the convent. I refuse to call it the Foundation of the Free Spirit — that's exactly what it wasn't! I need divers to drag that lake and someone who can crack the safe.'

'We've got a few blokes like that on the books, Jack,' joked Norman. 'Probably do it faster than the experts.'

Jack laughed. 'I dare say, but we need someone who isn't going to nick what's inside and leg it from force of habit.'

* * *

Once again, a convoy of police vehicles wound its way down the long drive to the convent of St Columbanus. As they passed the nuns' cemetery, Bugsy thought the good sisters would not have appreciated such frequent intrusion into their life of prayer and contemplation. On the other hand, they wouldn't have approved of what had been going on there, either. Was it fanciful to imagine they'd want the police to restore some kind of decency to the place?

Blimey, he thought, *get a grip Malone! All this supernatural non-sense is affecting your brain. Give me straightforward villains any day!*

The trawl of the convent and outbuildings took the best part of a week. The safe took some time to open, but inside they found huge wads of bank notes. It explained why Clive had been unable to find any unorthodox banking activity — like many other scams, the perpetrators insisted on cash. Lilith's laptop would reveal all the information on Charlie's stick, and more. They took it away along with the CCTV cameras from the Lodge and the one in the poker room.

'Now that Lilith's dead and beyond any criminal charges and Solomon's been officially classified as barmy, we don't really have anyone left to nick, do we, guv?' Bugsy sounded disappointed.

'No,' agreed Jack, 'but we do have a good clear-up rate. The old man will be pleased about that.'

'Lilith was poisonous, manipulative and downright evil,' said Aled. 'She ruined the lives of a lot of people.'

'You could argue,' said Gemma, dispassionate as ever, 'that if they hadn't got involved in the Black Mass and all the obscenities that went with it, they wouldn't haven't been targets for her crimes.'

'True,' agreed Bugsy. 'They were hardly innocent victims, apart from young Charlie. He was just doing his job.'

'Charlie was an ambitious young man with an attractive personality. He didn't deserve to die.' Georgia had come in from the hall, carrying a suitcase. 'Unlike my brother, who was too young to see what wickedness he was embroiled in. I'm afraid Solomon had convinced Perry that killing himself would make him a martyr, bring him closer to what he believed was the true religion — Satanism.' She looked at Jack. 'Is it all right if I go home to my father now, or do you need me to stay?'

'No, that's fine, Georgia. If we need anything more, we'll be in touch. I'm very sorry about the loss of your brother.'

'Thank you. At least now I have some knowledge of the circumstances surrounding his death. It's closure, but it will break my father's heart, all the same.' She looked sad and pale, but she smiled at the team and left to get into the taxi waiting outside.

'Lilith and Solomon might not have murdered the lad, but they might just as well have done.' Bugsy was angry. 'And they got away with it.'

'If the information on the laptop is as comprehensive as I believe it will be, we'll find irrefutable evidence that Lilith was responsible for the murders of Sir Bixby Carrington, Councillor Hughes-Jones and Charlie Updike. What we don't yet know is how much Bernie Bottle was involved.'

* * *

The lake gave up its contribution to the search for evidence.

'Look what the divers found, guv.' Bugsy indicated the haul of a metal wheelbarrow, a vintage gardening claw that the nuns had once used for cultivating, a man's clothes and shoes, and a lady's business suit, blouse, underwear and high-heeled shoes. There were also hypodermic syringes, a number of cloths once used for cleaning up blood and the remains of equipment associated with growing cannabis. 'Looks like when they saw us coming, they chucked all the incriminating stuff in the lake.'

'I wonder if it's still possible to get fingerprints from any of that?' said Jack. 'Let's consult the expert.'

Dr Hardacre was the oracle for all things forensic. Together with her team of scientists, she was always up to date with new developments and could be relied upon for an accurate opinion.

Bugsy showed her a photo of the wheelbarrow they had dredged up from the lake. It was true that people tended to chuck such rubbish into water rather than take the trouble to dispose of it responsibly, but in these circumstances, they were pretty certain it had been instrumental in a crime — possibly even two. They'd had to get the bodies of Sir Bixby and Amelia Hughes-Jones from the Foundation to the tomb in the forest somehow and a vehicle just wasn't an option.

'Doc, is it possible to recover fingerprints from a metal surface that's been submerged in water for some time?'

'Was it stagnant water, Sergeant?'

'It was in places. Does that make a difference?' asked Jack.

'Not necessarily. It just means that the duration of exposure to stagnant water defines the methods we use to enhance the prints and their subsequent quality.'

'D'you reckon your experts could find some on this wheelbarrow?'

'We'll certainly try, Sergeant. I'll give it a go with cyanoacrylate — a type of superglue that can undergo polymerization when it comes into contact with moisture in latent fingerprints. It's a forensic technique that we call "fuming". I can see your eyes beginning to glaze over, Sergeant. Just bring me the wheelbarrow and we'll take it from there.'

CHAPTER TWENTY-EIGHT

Clive and his team of techies had finally cracked the encryptions on the laptop. Jack called everyone to listen up. 'OK, what have you got for us?'

'This Lilith person was very careful about money. Looking at how she managed her files, I'd say it was all she really cared about. Her records are meticulous — every transaction, every person noted down in the online ledgers. Even her brother took second place to her control of the business. Obviously, there's nothing on here about that last Black Mass — she didn't stay alive long enough to cash up the takings. However, the many previous events made her shedloads of money.'

'Would that be from the "entry fee" she charged everyone?' asked Mitch.

'Not entirely. According to her online accounts, the real money came from the cash she extorted by blackmail.' He turned to Jack. 'There are loads of videos on here, sir, of indiscretions committed by prominent figures in business circles and in society. Many are readily recognizable. She must have hidden in the forest with a long lens to capture the detail. Obviously, we've kept them strictly confidential, but you'll know best how to dispose of them safely.'

'I rather think that will be one for the chief super or possibly even the commander,' hoped Jack.

'Then there's the matter of the illegal poker school. Evidence from the CCTV camera and transmitter shows Lilith cheated. She records that's how Sir Bixby lost his Rolex when he ran out of money to gamble with.'

'A watch that was last seen on Urbain's, aka Bernie Bottle's wrist,' said Gemma.

'What a piece of work!' exclaimed a constable in the front row.

'The most damning evidence was her detailed account of how she lured Sir Bixby down to the lake, drugged and drunk, then pushed him in.'

'I don't suppose she gave a reason?' asked Aled.

'She did, actually,' said Clive. 'She said he had challenged her one night, claiming to have a high-ranking friend in the police service and threatening to expose her.'

'Blimey, that would be Chief Superintendent Garwood,' muttered someone.

'She recorded then that she couldn't let him leave, lured him down to the lake and shoved him in. There's a similar account about how Councillor Mrs Hughes-Jones tried to grab some video evidence from her in the chapel, tripped on the steps in what she called "ridiculous stiletto heels" and cracked her head open. In both cases, she writes that Urbain disposed of their naked bodies by wheeling them into the forest and ripping their insides open with a cultivating implement. She says it was amusing that the *Echo* had described them as having been attacked by the Beast of Richington.'

'How daft to record everything,' observed Aled. 'Why would she do that?'

'Because she was proud of her ability to get the better of folk who believed themselves to be above her,' answered Malone. 'It was a narcissistic form of one-upmanship. It isn't uncommon in criminals.'

Jack was thinking about Georgia Delacour's brother. 'Clive, did you find anything more about Followers of the Enlightened Mind?'

'Sure did, sir. They operated out of a rural part of Hampshire. All the financial details relating to that enterprise were deleted so that even the lads in the tech team couldn't resurrect them. But she did mention the Honourable Peregrine Delacour being Solomon's Satanic apprentice. To quote her, she said, "*The stupid child actually believed in that Astaroth nonsense and hanged himself so that he could become a demon. Time to move on. I've found a suitable home for the next cult — the convent of St Columbanus in Kings Richington.*"'

The comments from the floor were predictable.

'What a callous cow!'

'You can say that again!'

'Pity she escaped justice by dying.'

'Pretty bloody selfish of her, I'd say.'

'It seems to me,' said Jack, 'that the conclusion of these findings puts the blame for these crimes solidly on the unholy trinity of Lilith, Solomon and Urbain. We aren't looking for anyone else.'

'It's a shame we didn't nail Bernie Bottle while we had him,' said Bugsy. 'CPS could push for murder by joint enterprise. At the very least, we could do him for drug dealing and unlawful disposal of two bodies.'

'We only have Lilith's account of that. He could deny it.'

'If Forensics find his fingerprints on the wheelbarrow and claw, I'd say we have a good case. He'll soon rise to the surface somewhere — scum always does.' Bugsy was confident.

'Top work, Clive,' said Jack.

'You know, boss, credit where it's due. This Lilith character was pretty good with technology and cameras. If she'd got a proper job, using her skills in a legal way, she could have made a packet without resorting to crime.'

'Maybe, but like the sergeant said, she wanted to prove how clever she was by outwitting the police and screwing money out of misguided folk who she thought were beneath her. It gave her more satisfaction than a proper job.'

* * *

The editor of the *Richington Echo* dunked a digestive biscuit in his tea and watched as half of it broke off and sank to the bottom. He wasn't surprised — it had been that kind of day. He was in something of a quandary. The image of the *Echo* as an independent, truth-seeking paper with a reputation for producing urgent, powerful, high-impact reporting had been somewhat tarnished by recent events. His paper, he claimed, had a strong sense of duty to the reader and the community. As the man in charge, he was editorially sympathetic to the underdog — anyone who felt oppressed by wealthy, intelligent, educated people — particularly if it gave him the opportunity to have a pop at the police, the government and the local council. His quandary was that he couldn't quite equate that with recent articles.

The Beast of Richington Forest stories had sold a mountain of copies, supported by his criticism of the police for refusing to take appropriate action to catch it and for the delay in formally identifying the victims, despite the *Echo* asking anyone with information to come forward. The 'beast' had turned out to be a hoax.

The photograph of Summer Johnson's innocent baby face on the front page had tugged at everyone's heartstrings. The editorial had asked readers to help identify the missing child who was lost and at risk, only to discover later that she had murdered her parents and her grandparents. Some innocent baby!

Following his drinking buddy's account of obscene goings-on in the forest, the *Echo* had supported the council's view that an exorcism should be held to cleanse the evil that was clearly lurking there, hoping to get full coverage in the process. As it turned out, the old priest had died in the attempt and the reporter who had covered the exorcism

— Charlie Updike — had himself been killed, while working undercover in the cult.

It had been a final blow to discover that the *Echo* had been unknowingly running invites for the Black Mass in its personal column. A centre-page spread of that final mass, with the police charging in mob-handed with tasers, guns and dogs would have been magnificent. The downside was that many of the 'disciples' who had dropped their robes in panic and ran around naked were the same worthy citizens who donated large sums to keep the *Echo* going. The announcement from the police press office was bland. It stated that arrests had been made and no further illegal activities in the forest were expected. All in all, it had not been a successful summer. He turned off his computer and went down to the Richington Arms to drown his sorrows.

* * *

'Good news, guv.' Bugsy was in high spirits, due partly to a report from the Strathclyde Police and partly because he'd just demolished a foot-long bacon and egg roll and two yum-yums.

'Tell me,' said Jack. 'I could do with cheering up.' He paused, frowning. 'It's bloody hot in here.'

'It's autumn, sir,' said Mitch. 'That time of year when, apart from messing about with the clocks, the heating is switched on remotely by HQ. The problem is that it's stuck on high. We've called the engineers and they said they'd be here on Monday.'

'Yeah, but they didn't say which Monday, did they?' complained Aled, loosening his shirt collar.

'What did the report from Strathclyde say, Sarge?' Gemma was fanning herself with a copy of *Police Life*.

'They've traced Bernie Bottle to Glasgow. He's calling himself Willie Cameron. The dozy sod tried to pawn the Rolex. Would you believe he could be that stupid, guv?'

'Yes, I would. Otherwise we shouldn't have been able to put him inside so many times.'

'The pawnbroker smelled a rat when she saw the engraving, "*To my darling Bixby on our silver wedding anniversary.*" She reckoned it was a knock-off and told Bernie to come back after she'd had a chance to value it. She rang the police. They matched his prints to the ones on the database and picked him up. Apparently, he'd already started up a lucrative drug dealing racket and he's likely to be spending the next couple of Hogmanays in Barlinnie.'

'So much for "Urbain, the Liberal Science Guru",' said Mitch. 'Now he's just Bernie the Berk of Barlinnie.'

'If Doctor Hardacre can get his prints off the wheelbarrow and the farm claw, and we can prove he was implicated in the murders, he'll be going away for a lot longer than a couple of years,' decided Jack.

'It's good that Sir Bixby's wife can have his Rolex back, though.' Gemma wasn't much into sentimental values but she could understand that it would be important to Jenny Mackintosh. A keepsake from happier times.

'I'll let Chief Superintendent Garwood know,' said Jack. 'He'll want to return it personally.'

Aled returned from the direction of the men's lavatory. 'Sarge, there's a terrible stink coming from the gents'.'

'There's *always* a terrible stink coming from the gents',' observed Gemma. 'It's because you're all a bunch of filthy animals with no concept of hygiene.'

'Harsh — very harsh,' chastised Bugsy.

Aled shook his head. 'No, seriously, it's foul. Like something putrid is decaying in there.'

'It's probably the drains,' observed Mitch. 'I'll get the environmental people to look into it.'

CHAPTER TWENTY-NINE

'Now that things have quietened down a bit, I thought we'd have some people over for drinks and a buffet supper on Wednesday evening.' Corrie was already planning the food in her head.

'Why Wednesday?' Jack looked up from the bulb catalogue that he was browsing. 'Why not at the weekend?'

Corrie sighed. 'In case you hadn't noticed, I run a catering company and the weekend is my busiest time. Wednesdays are pretty quiet.' She went to fetch some glasses and a bottle of what she considered to be a rather cheeky little Sancerre that she'd had chilling in the fridge. She glanced over his shoulder. 'What are you doing with a bulb catalogue?'

'I thought I'd plant a few tulips for next spring. Brighten up that flower bed in the front garden.'

Corrie sniffed. 'What about the bulbs you stored in the garage last year?'

'They went all flat and black during the winter.'

'Only because you kept running over them in the car. I don't want to discourage you, sweetheart, but what you know about gardening I could write on a bay leaf.'

Jack was offended. 'I'll have you know, true gardeners grow at the speed of oak trees, not mustard and cress.'

'Who told you that?' Corrie giggled.

'Howard and Harriet from the Foundation. They've transformed that convent garden. It looks amazing, and they grow so much of their own fruit and vegetables. Then there are the chickens for eggs and the goats for yogurt and cheese. It'll be a real shame if they have to leave.'

Corrie sipped her wine, thoughtfully. 'What *will* happen to them, now that the Foundation has folded? They were doing such a good job looking after the young, vulnerable members.'

'I know. They're good people. I really believe they had no idea about the evil that was going on right under their noses.'

'I hope someone will step in and put some weight behind the future of the convent. Cynthia and I thought it was such a peaceful environment.'

'Who are you planning to invite to this bash on Wednesday?' Jack hoped it wouldn't be the Garwoods. The old man had been behaving even more strangely than usual and he wasn't really a party animal.

'Professor MacDuff and Marigold Catwater for a start. Such complex, interesting people. Bugsy and Iris, obviously, and Carlene and Antoine have offered to help with the food.'

'Do you think we might invite Howard and Harriet? They're not under suspicion and they've already provided witness statements — not that they witnessed anything relevant. They're still upset about Charlie Updike.'

Corrie smiled to herself. Jack really was an old softie when it came to people who were out of luck through no fault of their own. 'Of course we can, sweetheart. They can give you some advice on your flattened tulip bulbs. That's ten including us. We need two more to make up the dozen.

'How about DC Williams and DC Fox? The last few weeks have been pretty character-building for them. They've coped very well since young Aled went off like a two-bob firework on an investigation of his own without reporting in first. But I think he's learned a valuable lesson about teamwork and always watching your back.'

'Why not? They'll provide some younger company for Carlene and Antoine.' She took a big mouthful of the Sancerre and swilled it around. 'How would you describe this wine? I'd call it mouth-filling.'

Jack took a mouthful and pulled a face. 'I'd call it buttock-clenching.'

* * *

On Monday morning at eight o'clock sharp, the engineer arrived to fix the heating. Bugsy was impressed with his appearance and his efficient approach. His only experience of itinerant workmen was back in the days when a bloke would turn up wearing grubby overalls, whistling tunelessly, with a pencil behind his ear and a battered toolbox. Before any work was attempted, the conversation would start with, 'Three sugars, ta very much, them chocolate hob-nobs look tasty, what about Tottenham bloomin' Hotspur last Saturday, flippin' diabolical, any luck on the gee-gees?' and so on.

Nothing remotely like that these days. The engineer was smartly dressed in a suit with the company logo on the pocket. Bugsy had come in early to explain that the heating was stuck on 'bloody tropical' and could he please turn it down to 'moderately British'? The engineer set about the task in hand immediately, never mind a pause for tea and biscuits. After a good deal of tapping away on his laptop and checking Smart thermostats and user input settings, the engineer declared, somewhat haughtily, that he could find nothing wrong with the system.

'The temperature, sir, is in line with acceptable heating parameters for an office space of this size. I have to say, it doesn't feel particularly tropical to me.'

Bugsy realized then that over the weekend, it had indeed returned to normal. 'Must've been a blip, mate. Sorry we called you out.' The engineer left wondering whether law and order in Kings Richington was safe in the hands of coppers who didn't know if they were hot or cold.

Next day, the environmental plumber arrived to deal with the stink in the gents'. Aled was surprised to open the security door to a young lady carrying a briefcase instead of the bloke with drain rods and jetting hoses that he'd been expecting. He felt he should apologize in advance of escorting her into the gents'.

'Sorry about the terrible pong. We think the sewage must have backed up.'

She smiled at him. 'Don't worry, sir. I've smelled them all in my time — floor drain dysfunction, defective U-bend traps, grout mould. Could be you just need a urinal cake to soak up the smell of the urine that isn't being flushed away. We'll soon get to the bottom of it, no pun intended.'

Aled opened the door for her and they went inside. She inhaled deeply. Then she did it again. 'I don't know about you, sir, but all I can smell is air freshener. Hawaiian hibiscus, if I'm not much mistaken.'

Aled took a big breath. She was right. The stink, like the faulty heating, had apparently disappeared miraculously overnight. 'I'm so sorry. It seems to be OK now, but thanks for coming.'

Needless to say, Garwood complained about the cost of calling out expensive operatives for no reason. 'You don't hear me whimpering about minor inconveniences. I just get on with fixing it myself.' However, he changed his mind when he switched on his computer to check the monthly returns and nothing happened. He burst into the main office. 'Dawes, my computer's dead. Can't get the blasted thing to work. How am I going to see whether the station is hitting its targets without my spreadsheets? Get your technology nerd onto it.'

Clive hurried down the corridor to Garwood's office, only to return less than five minutes later. 'It's working fine, sir.'

Garwood was impressed. 'Good man.' He turned on Jack. 'You see, Dawes? That's what I call efficiency. None of this calling people in for no reason. Just needs someone who knows what he's doing.' He blustered out.

'What was wrong with it, Clive?' asked Bugsy.

'Nothing, Sarge. I switched it on and it fired up straight away. Some sort of glitch, I imagine.'

'We've had a few strange glitches lately,' observed Aled. 'Things that aren't working properly one minute, then mysteriously fix themselves. If I didn't know better, I'd say—'

'Well don't, son. We've had enough of devils and demons and things that go bump in the night. It's all bollocks. What is it?'

'It's all bollocks, Sarge!' everyone chorused.

CHAPTER THIRTY

The buffet party turned out to be just what everyone needed. Howard and Harriet had some exciting news that they were eager to share.

'We've been awarded some funding from the council,' explained Howard. 'They're going to put plans in place for us to run the old convent as a halfway house for youngsters who are coming out of care into the community.'

'It was when we found out about poor Charlie being brought up in a children's home that we got the idea,' added Harriet. 'Some young people aren't ready to live independently when they're that young.'

'We thought that we could teach them some skills like growing your own food, how to cook and generally looking after themselves.'

'Will it just be you two?' asked Corrie.

'Surprisingly, Gideon has agreed to stay. He feels he could add some value regarding medical education and first aid, even though he isn't allowed to practise any more. He didn't explain why but he said he owed it to one child in particular. I got the feeling he might have lost one who was important to him.'

'That's really good.' Corrie was delighted. 'We wondered what would happen to those susceptible cult members when there was no one there to guide them.'

'Mae and Goliath are coming back to convalesce for a while. They will be immensely helpful. Mae will teach the youngsters to enjoy different kinds of music and Gollie will just love them all. Something they may not have had enough of in their short lives.'

'Rushil still drifts silently about the grounds in a spiritual world of his own,' added Harriet. 'He's offered free yoga and meditation to our young people, which might be just what some of the more disturbed ones need.'

Over by the buffet table, Professor MacDuff and Marigold were enjoying Antoine's *mousse de saumon* canapés. Aled approached, diffidently. 'Professor, I haven't been able to speak to you since the . . . er . . .' He was struggling.

'Since the fiasco in the forest?' helped MacDuff.

'That's right. I just wanted to say thank you. If it hadn't been for you, I think I'd have been done for.'

'Think nothing of it, DC Williams. We elderly academics are of little use in the modern world but occasionally we can justify the air we breathe.'

There was something Carlene had been wanting to ask the Professor ever since that night he had put an end to the Black Mass. She decided to ask him now.

'Professor, when you were banishing the evil powers and asking God to protect us in the battle, you looked like you were rising up off the tomb. How did you do that?'

'I saw that, too,' agreed Corrie. 'It looked like a kind of levitation.'

MacDuff smiled. 'I think it must have been a trick of the light, ladies. It was difficult to see anything clearly. I was simply pulling myself up to my full height.'

Corrie and Carlene exchanged glances. They knew what they had seen, but they didn't push it. Could it be that this remarkable man really did have God on his side?

At the other end of the table, Bugsy and Iris were helping themselves to what, for them, was haute cuisine. Iris described herself as a good, plain cook, which was fine, because Bugsy had a good, plain appetite.

'What are these, Antoine?' he asked, picking up a shell. 'They look like whelks. I'm partial to a whelk.' He picked one up, forked out the contents and sucked it into his mouth before Iris could caution him.

'They are not whelks, Monsieur Bugsy,' replied Antoine. 'They are *escargots à la Bourguignonne.*'

'I knew that,' said Bugsy, instantly. Then, more quietly: 'What exactly does that mean?'

'Snails in garlic herb butter,' explained Carlene. 'They're an acquired taste, Sergeant Bugsy.'

'In that case, I'll acquire another one. Don't let anyone accuse me of being a food snob. I'll eat snails along with the rest of 'em. If they're good enough for hedgehogs, they're good enough for me.' He had a sudden thought. 'You don't eat hedgehogs in France, do you, son?'

Antoine laughed. 'Non, Monsieur Bugsy. Not since the sixteenth century.'

* * *

Aled and Gemma had piled up their plates and were sitting on the stairs to eat.

Aled glanced sideways at Gemma. 'I'm sorry about . . . you know . . . about going off at half-cock and getting you involved. It was irresponsible and stupid. It isn't what we were trained to do and it would serve me right if I get demoted back to uniform.' He paused. 'Sometimes I think Mam and Tad were right. I should have been a rugby player not a police officer.'

Gemma elbowed him in the ribs and he spilled ketchup, sneaked from a kitchen cupboard, down the front of his new shirt. 'Stop feeling sorry for yourself! OK, you made a mistake.

The person who never made a mistake never made anything. You're a bloody good copper, Aled — brave, hard-working and intuitive. Don't let anyone tell you otherwise. And as for rugby players — any big, hard hooligan can put on a stripey shirt and barge into people. I've seen them in the pub — all gobby when someone gets in their way at the bar, then they can't hold their drink and try it on women miles out of their league when the beer kicks in. Your only problem, my little Welsh cake, is that you can get yourself into trouble marginally faster than you can run away from it. Now put that *pissaladière* down and give me a kiss.'

* * *

As the evening drew to a close, everyone sat in the drawing room drinking coffee. Jack was handing out glasses of Armagnac to the guests who weren't driving. The conversation became philosophical and serious.

'No demons in that place after all, Professor. Just an ordinary bunch of crooks,' said Bugsy.

Alistair MacDuff shook his head. 'On the contrary, Sergeant, that place was teeming with demons of every kind.'

Bugsy was puzzled. 'How d'you make that out, Prof?'

'Think about it. Solomon's demons were real enough — in his head. Real enough for him to kill his sister to ingratiate himself into their favour. All those misguided people at the Black Mass clearly had demons in their souls, otherwise why did they feel the need to be there, doing what they were doing?'

'Gideon has demons,' agreed Jack. 'I doubt he'll ever be rid of them, but working with young people at the convent might help him to live with them. Georgia's brother, Perry, believed in demons to the extent that he hanged himself in order to join them. At least now his family have closure in the knowledge that those responsible for driving him to it are either dead or locked up.'

'I assisted Doctor Hardacre with the post-mortems on the grandparents of that young girl, Summer Johnson,' recalled Marigold. 'I remember saying to Alistair that to do that to people who loved her and cared for her must indicate evil possession of some kind.'

'She said her demons told her to do it,' added Bugsy. 'They'd been with her all her life and she had to do what the voices told her — that included setting fire to the house and killing her parents when she was ten. I doubt you can be more possessed by evil than that.'

'Mae's demons were not of her own making,' said Gemma, 'but at least now she won't have to spend the rest of her life looking over her shoulder for them.'

'I don't think Len and Trottie had any demons, did they, Harriet?' asked Howard.

'I don't think they had the wits, quite honestly. I doubt either of them ever had an original thought in their lives, let alone something as complicated as a demon.'

'What about Urbain, alias Bernie Bottle, the drug dealer?' asked Aled. 'Incidentally, sir, you'll be pleased to hear that Doctor Hardacre was able to lift latent fingerprints from the wheelbarrow. They're good enough quality to be a match so we have evidence to support what Lilith recorded on her laptop. He did use it to transport the two bodies from the convent to the forest. There are enough traces on the claw to show it was Bottle who ripped out their insides, so we can prove he was implicated in the murders.'

'I doubt he had enough of a conscience to have any personal demons,' said Bugsy. 'But drugs would certainly incite them in the addicts he sold them to. Filthy way to make a living.'

'Why did they have to kill Charlie?' asked Harriet. 'His only demon — if you can call it that — was ambition. He wanted to be a top journalist.'

Jack was thoughtful. 'Charlie was a victim of Lilith's demons. Her greed and avarice had overwhelmed any scruples or morals she may once have had. She was prepared to do anything for money — even murder. That's evil isn't it, Professor?'

211

'Indeed, it is,' he agreed. 'Demons aren't all about the black arts and summoning the devil. There is a great deal more to evocation than Solomon's cheap conjuring tricks like his contact lenses that glow in the dark and green, chemically-induced vapours dribbling from his nostrils, never mind the stunt with the flash paper that made flames appear from the devil's figurine.'

'How do you know about all that stuff, Professor?' asked Corrie. 'Solomon couldn't do most of his special effects at the Black Mass we attended, because of the rain.'

'I have my spies, dear lady. If I've learned one thing about demonology, it's that you don't meddle with it if you're not fully prepared. And as I believe I once told you, Jack, demons can take many forms. Human nature is essentially weak, errant and susceptible to demonic temptation. It's because of this that servants of the devil can seriously harm people by occult. We underestimate them at our peril.'

EPILOGUE

After the police had removed him from the scene of his sister's murder, Solomon had undergone weeks of assessment by court-appointed psychiatrists of some experience. They eventually declared him psychotic, the conclusion being that he had no conscious choice of action due to his illness. Their unanimous recommendation was that he was unfit to stand trial and should be detained for an indefinite period in a high-security psychiatric unit, with round-the-clock monitoring. Any chance of recovery from his condition was remote. He would remain in detention for the rest of his life as he represented a high degree of harm to himself and others. He had refused any form of therapy or psychology-based treatment, claiming that Astaroth would soon facilitate his release and they would all burn in hell.

In his crisis stabilization unit in a hospital for the criminally insane, Solomon was chuckling to himself. What excellent mischief he had wrought with the help of the Grand Duke of Hell. His only regret was that the fools would not realize that it was the devil's work. No matter. He had plans to show them that would leave them in no doubt. Once he was out of this place of profound and nauseating incorruptibility, he would redress the balance between evil and good. First on his list would be the sanctimonious Professor MacDuff.

Astaroth had numbered him among the serpents to be condemned to eternal damnation. With his newly acquired powers of depravity and manipulation, Solomon was confident of success. He stood tall, two fingers on each hand pointing up and two pointing down — the devil's horns. He chanted, '*Ave Satanas. Ave Astaroth.*'

Watching him on the CCTV camera, the nurse working the night shift on his twenty-four-hour observation was unconcerned. It was recorded in his notes that this patient would perform this routine anything up to twenty times a day. Any attempt to discourage this behaviour caused him to become stressed and violent, so it was deemed in the patient's interest to allow it. Psychiatrists were hopeful that the frequency would diminish in time. The nurse looked away briefly to speak to a colleague. When he looked back, Solomon was rolling on the floor, clutching at his throat and gasping for breath. The nurse pressed the panic alarm and ran down the corridor towards Solomon's room.

* * *

Detective Inspector Dawes and Detective Sergeant Malone had been for an end-of-investigation drink in the Richington Arms with the rest of the MIT. It was dark as they were walking home, slightly the worse for wear, but the moon was full. The entire team was relieved at the conclusion of what had been a harrowing few weeks.

'I don't know about you, Jack, but I'm glad all that "devils and demons" stuff's over. Give me a straightforward murder any day. I can just about cope with women who bump off their husbands for their money or blokes who strangle their wives in a jealous rage.'

'I agree, but the professor would claim they're also battling demons.'

'Yeah, maybe.' Bugsy was still doubtful.

They were passing the end of the drive that led to the convent when Jack stopped. 'Bugsy, can you see figures walking — or rather floating — towards the convent?'

'Not funny, Jack. I know I've had a couple of pints but I'm not . . .' He paused. 'Bloody hell, guv. Yes, I can.'

'What do they look like to you?'

'Not Black Mass disciples in hooded robes, that's for sure. We've put a stop to that nonsense. They don't look like members of the cult, either. They look more like . . .'

'Nuns,' said Jack, shortly.

'But there aren't any nuns in the convent now. Haven't been for years. D'you think we should go and investigate?'

'I doubt we'd see anything if we did.' Jack decided. 'Probably just shadows in the moonlight.'

'Yeah, that'll be it,' said Bugsy, unconvinced. 'I mean — it won't be phantoms of the nuns returning to reclaim their convent, now that the demons have been driven out, will it?'

'Course not,' said Jack. 'Come on, let's cut through the forest. Time we were home. Corrie and Iris will be worrying.'

They'd just reached the clearing where the tomb stood when Bugsy said, 'Jack, can you smell something 'orrible?'

Jack sniffed. 'Yeah. I expect you've trodden in something.'

Bugsy looked down at his shoes. 'I didn't think fox shit smelled as bad as this.'

At that moment, the moon emerged from behind the clouds and sent two piercing beams of light through gaps in the trees. Close by, an animal howled.

Jack looked at Bugsy. 'Might this be a good time to practise the shuttle run for the police fitness test?'

'Absolutely.'

They broke into a vigorous jog.

* * *

By the time they reached Solomon's room and unlocked the security doors, he was choking. Despite every effort, they were unable to resuscitate him. They recorded his last gagging words for the benefit of the inevitable inquest.

'Avenging nuns. Astaroth! Save me!'

THE END

Thank you for reading this book. If you enjoyed it please leave a review on Amazon or Goodreads.

We love to hear from our readers. If there is anything we missed or you have a question about then please get in touch: feedback@joffebooks.com

Join our mailing list to get new releases and great deals every week from one of the UK's leading independent publishers.

www.joffebooks.com

Made in the USA
Monee, IL
16 October 2021